William Richardson

Remarks on Diabetes

Anatiposi

William Richardson

Remarks on Diabetes

Reprint of the original.

1st Edition 2023 | ISBN: 978-3-38210-237-1

Anatiposi Verlag is an imprint of Outlook Verlagsgesellschaft mbH.

Verlag (Publisher): Outlook Verlag GmbH, Zeilweg 44, 60439 Frankfurt, Deutschland
Vertretungsberechtigt (Authorized to represent): E. Roepke, Zeilweg 44, 60439 Frankfurt, Deutschland
Druck (Print): Books on Demand GmbH, In de Tarpen 42, 22848 Norderstedt, Deutschland

REMARKS

ON

DIABETES

ESPECIALLY WITH REFERENCE TO TREATMENT

BY

WILLIAM RICHARDSON, M.A., M.D.

MEMBER OF THE ROYAL COLLEGE OF PHYSICIANS, LONDON.

LONDON:

H. K. LEWIS, 136 GOWER STREET, W.C.

1871.

PREFACE.

TEN years ago the author of this little work was attacked with Diabetes which presented symptoms of a very formidable character. He entirely treated himself, and, after the failure of every remedy, dietetic and medical, which he found recommended on good authority, was gradually led to the method of treatment he advises in the following pages. He has not only cured himself, but also many others who have faithfully and patiently carried out the system he advocates. The author repeats, *faithfully and patiently*, for he has found some difficulty in inducing patients to carry it out in its integrity. Some object to the bath, as involving much domestic inconvenience, and exposing to the danger of colds, etc., while others, overcome by the feeling of lassitude and weakness peculiar to the disease, consider themselves incapable of taking the walking exercise essential to recovery. With such feelings the author can fully sympathise, as he experienced them to an extreme degree. These objections must not, however, be entertained by him who desires relief. The bath and walking exercise are of peculiar importance in the treatment, so much so, that if either is neglected, but little good will result.

To fairly test the system of treatment it must be carried out as a whole, in fact the gradual relaxation of the diet without the exercise would be positively injurious.

The drugs recommended are few, but if employed as directed, they will be found an essential part of the treatment. The author did not get clear of sugar till he used them. It will be seen that the doses are small; irritation from their necessarily long use is thus avoided, a point the author thinks not sufficiently attended to in the treatment of chronic diseases.

25 Gloucester Gardens, London. W.
March, 1871.

CONTENTS.

REMARKS ON DIABETES.

CHAPTER I.

HISTORY, ETC.

THE name diabetes is derived from a Greek word, διαβαινειν, signifying "to pass through," from the abundance of urine which is a special symptom of this disease. The term Glycosuria (γλυκυς, sweet, οὐρον, urine) has been proposed to be substituted for Diabetes by M. Bouchardat; and though it has the advantage of indicating what is an essential character of the malady—for no one would consider a case diabetic without the presence of sugar in the urine—yet it is to be remembered that the ancients knew nothing of this symptom, and they gave the name Diabetes to a certain assemblage of symptoms, of which the most prominent were increased secretion of urine, thirst, dry skin, gradual emaciation and loss of strength; again, as sugar, and often in considerable quantity, is present in the urine of patients, without any of these general symptoms, and also occasionally in those suffering from such diseases as congestion of the liver, diseased heart, or lungs, epileptic fits, gout etc., it is better to retain the name Diabetes for those cases, where with the presence of sugar in the urine general symptoms exist, and to limit the term Glycosuria to those cases where sugar is present in the urine unaccompanied by general symptoms and which, therefore, would not be treated as cases of Diabetes; the presence of the sugar being considered as an accidental complication, arising, most probably, from disturbance of the functions of the liver.

In giving a short history of the various theories that have been formed as to the nature of this disease, I shall confine myself chiefly to those which have suggested new modes of treatment, which, from the advantages derived, have outlived the theories from which they originated.

The ancients designated every disease by the name of Diabetes in which with an increase of urine there was thirst, progressive wasting and loss of strength; but as they were almost entirely unacquainted with Pathological Anatomy and Chemistry, Diabetes was placed by them under the class of diseases called

"Phthisis," which included all diseases the main characteristic of which was wasting, the cause of the wasting making no difference as to the classification.

The chemical theories, as to the nature of Diabetes, date from the observations of Willis, who, in 1674 noticed that the urine of a diabetic patient had a sweet flavour. Cowley in 1778 separated the sugar from the urine. Dr. Rollo in his work on Diabetes (1797-8) argued that from the symptoms and effects it consisted in a disorder of the stomach proceeding from a morbid change in the powers of digestion and assimilation; that this change consisted in an increased action and secretion with vitiation of the gastric juice, and probably of too active a state of the lacteal absorbents; that the sugar of the disease is formed in the stomach chiefly, if not entirely, from the vegetable matter taken as food, and that the kidneys and other parts of the system, as the skin, are affected secondarily. He therefore conceived that cutting off all the supplies of vegetable matter taken as food was the rational mode of treatment, hereby laying the foundation of the restriction of diet, which at the present time is still most beneficially employed. Dr. Rollo considered that by regimen and medicine you could prevent the formation of sugar, and diminish the increased action of the heart, and that the best means to effect this object were repose, an entire abstinence from vegetable matter and the use of emetics, narcotics etc.

Early in this century Nicolas and Gaudeville looked on this disease as arising from an intestinal affection, in consequence of which the chyle instead of being composed of nitrogenous matter, consisted of less perfectly elaborated elements of. saccharine matter and not fitted for the nutrition of the body.

In 1837 McGregor detected sugar in the blood; he also discovered it in the matter vomitted by a diabetic patient, who had been fed for three days on roast beef and water: he, therefore, considered as Rollo did, that the fault was in the digestive organs; that what ought to be converted into healthy chyle was changed into saccharine matter and, entering into the circulation, was excreted by the kidneys.

Supported by the authority of Rollo, Nicolas, and Gaudeville, M. Bouchardat (*Annuaire* 1841) gave the following views of Diabetes. The existence of sugar in the urine has its origin in the transformation of amylaceous matter, taken as food, into sugar such as we can effect in our laboratory, that there exists in diabetes a principle which has on starch an action similar to that of diastase: he further asserted that in all the diabetic patients he had seen, the quantity of sugar contained in the urine was in direct ratio to the quantity of starchy aliment and sugar they took; if the quantity of amylaceous elements and sugar was diminished, the quantity of sugar in the urine was diminished in like proportion: that the thirst of a diabetic patient is always in direct ratio to the sugar and amylaceous matter taken: he observed, he says further, that for a quantity of food representing a pound of starchy matter the patient drank ordinarily about twelve pints of water and passed about fourteen pints of urine: he explained the ardent thirst which torments the patient by a fact which is well known chemically, that for the complete change of starchy matter into sugar it must be dissolved in about seven times its weight of water; a similar phenomenon takes place in the diabetic patient in order that the transformation of starch into sugar may take place, hence the terrible, irresistible thirst. In a memoir published in 1846, he says, on causing a diabetic patient to vomit one hour after a meal of starch, and examining the vomited matter, he found sugar; by further analysis he discovered a substance composed of Oxygen, Hydrogen, Carbon, and Nitrogen, which he considered to be the diastase, capable of transposing starch into sugar in the stomach: on the contrary, in a sound man, the vomited matter contained no such substance two hours after a repast of starchy matter, and a very small proportion of glucon or sugar. In *Annuaire* 1846 (supplement p. 199), he considered that the digestion of a diabetic patient differed from that of a sound man in that the transformation of amylaceous matter in the one was rapid, taking place in the stomach, whilst in the latter it was slow, taking place in the intestines; and that the principal cause of diabetes was an abundant use of amylaceous matter, and a more rapid formation of sugar with its consequent introduction into the circulation, more being absorbed at one time than can be assimilated. I have enlarged upon the views both of Dr. Rollo and M. Bouchardat, as I consider them representatives, the one in England, the other in France, of the stomachic origin of diabetes, and it is wonderful how closely their dietetic treatment of the disease corresponds. Bouchardat introduced into France the system of dieting the patient, from which great benefit was derived; he also invented a gluten bread which goes by his name and is the diabetic bread in use there. By this treatment,—the complete abstinence from sugar and starch,—Bouchardat said, in 1838, that after twelve hours the thirst abated, the urine gradually became normal, the appetite restrained within its ordinary limits, and the health became re-established. But in 1841 we find him speaking very differently, for he confesses that three patients, whom he had considered cured, died; and what showed also that the sugar in diabetes had another source than the starch and sugar taken as food, was the relation by M. Leblanc, veterinary surgeon, at a meeting of the Academy of Medicine, of the case of a dog six and a half years old, which had been fed all its life on raw beef and yet suffered from diabetes. Dr. Prout, however, states that he never saw a case of diabetes in one of the lower animals.

But the question was soon asked why it was, since sugar and amylaceous food are constantly taken, the diabetic patient alone eliminated sugar. The same answer was given by M. Mialhe (*Academie des Sciences*, 1843), and M. Alvaro Reynoso (*Memoire sur la presence du sucre dans les urines*, Victor Masson, 1853). Mialhe said that sugar was destroyed in a sound organism by the alkalinity of the blood, but that in a diabetic patient the blood is too little alkaline, or even acid, and so the sugar could not be destroyed; this was the origin of the alkaline plan of treatment, to increase or restore the alkalinity of the blood; it was the consequence of Mialhe's theory, and though this theory is wrong as to the reaction of the blood, for it has been proved that the serum of the blood in diabetes is as alkaline as that of healthy blood, and that even a fluid more alkaline than the blood could not decompose glucon, yet the treatment has been followed by very remarkable results. Valleix says of this theory, that it is as complete, as satisfactory to the mind, as is permitted man to make; it is also to be looked upon as founded upon the sure basis of facts. *(Bulletin de Therapeutique,* 1845 Vol. xxx.*)*

M. Alvaro Reynoso considered that the sugar was destroyed in the healthy organism by respiration, basing it upon what he considered a proved fact that sugar was contained in the blood before its passage through the lungs, but that after that none was found. Diabetes, according to this theory, depends upon deficient respiration, he therefore advocated a stimulant plan of treatment so as to increase the respiratory function.

We now come to a period when the chemical origin and theories based upon it ceased to be urged, and its origin from nerve lesions to be advocated. For this change we are entirely indebted to M. Claude Bernard, who in *Archives Generales de Medecin*, 1848, announced the remarkable fact "that sugar was formed in the liver as a normal process in all animals, and that this formation occurred independently of diet, in carnivorous, as well as in herbivorous animals, and that its production was confined to the liver. He showed also that lesions of the nerve centres caused sugar to appear in the urine; by wounding the floor of the fourth ventricle he could produce temporarily sugar in the urine from disturbance of the vaso-motor nerves, and so causing an acceleration of the hepatic circulation. In 1857 he discovered in the liver the matter from which the sugar was formed calling it Glycogenic matter (the Amyloid matter of Pavy). He seemed to have based his theory upon so secure a foundation that there did not appear to be a shadow of doubt as to its truth. Considering, therefore, diabetes to arise from a natural and physiological function of the liver, either from direct irritation or, indirectly, from irritation of the nerves (for he has made known to us a nervous form of diabetes), the treatment was recommended in accordance with this theory, at one time sedative, at another by means capable of acting upon the nervous system, as a seton to the nape of the neck, Bromide of Potassium, Electricity, etc.

This theory of diabetes by Bernard was considered an established fact until the publication of Dr. Pavy's book on the *Nature and Treatment of Diabetes* in 1862, who denied the power of the liver to form sugar, and considered the formation of this principle as a postmortem result, the nervous system during life preventing its formation. M. Schiff corroborated Dr. Pavy's experiments and a new theory was formed by them of Diabetes which has been called "The theory of Ferments." According to this the Glycogenitic matter, called by Dr. Pavy Amyloid matter, contained in the liver is changed into sugar by the action of a substance analogous to "diastase;" this substance, according to Dr. Pavy, always exists, but is prevented from acting during life by nervous influence; but immediately after death on the withdrawal of nervous influence its action takes place, sugar is thus formed and hence diabetes. Schiff denies the existence of diastase in the liver in its normal state; he considers that it is formed after death and not only in the hepatic blood but also in the blood of the general circulation. According to him, the liver is the centre of the diabetic phenomenon, viz. the formation of sugar, but it is a passive centre, the ferment, or diastase formed in any part of the circulation becoming efficacious in the liver; indeed in order to form the ferment, Schiff considered it was only necessary to put an obstacle in the way of the general circulation, thus he put a ligature round the arm of a man whose urine gave no signs of sugar, he tightened the ligature so as to produce almost complete paralysis of motion and sensibility, the urine voided half an hour after gave decided evidence of the presence of sugar. The augmentation of the ferment has not been demonstrated any more than the ferment itself; further, there are cases of disturbance of circulation without fever in which sugar does not occur in the urine, such as heart affections, congestion of lungs, &c. Schiff proved by experiment that excess of sugar in the blood arises from some modification of the function of the liver; he extirpated the liver of frogs and on examining their blood three weeks after found no sugar. It seems proved by this experiment that pricking the floor of the 4th ventricle does not produce sugar in the blood without the intervention of the liver, and in fact that the liver is the organ by which sugar is formed; he also showed, as M. Claude Bernard had done before, by tying portions of the liver in frogs previously rendered Glycosuric, that the quantity of sugar in the urine diminished in proportion to the diminution of the volume of the liver; hereby confirming the view that the liver is the organ through which Glycosuria or Diabetes has its origin. (Trousseau's *Clinical Medicine*. Vol. 3. Page 517.)

Dr. Flint of New York, the writer of the *Physiology of Man*, undertook some experiments on animals to endeavour to reconcile the conflicting opinions of M. Cl. Bernard and Dr. Pavy. He says very truly "it is difficult to understand how any observer so well known and accurate as Dr. Pavy could assert positively, as the result of personal examination, that the liver does not contain sugar when examined immediately after its removal from the living animal whilst Cl. Bernard and so many others have demonstrated its presence in large quantities;" yet such was the result of all the experiments of Dr. Pavy, and the same conclusion was arrived at by Dr. McDonnell, Meissner, Sæger, and Schiff. As the result of his experiments there seems to be no doubt that the liver in a living animal contains no sugar, agreeing thus with Dr. Pavy;

but he differs from him in this respect, that though no sugar is found in the liver yet it is formed by the liver, being he considers washed away by the blood into the hepatic veins as fast as it is formed; his experiments shew how very quickly after death sugar is formed by the liver. This conclusion was founded on the fact that though only meat was taken as food, yet when an extract was made from the blood of the Portal vein and from the substance of the liver no sugar was found in them, although an extract made from the blood of the Hepatic vein always indicated the presence of sugar. He considered, and I think rightly, that this sugar could only be derived from a sugar-forming function of the liver, for as no sugar is found in the Vena Porta, nor in the liver when examined quickly after death, but is always met with in the hepatic veins, it is impossible to conceive that the sugar is derived from any other source than the liver,* thus establishing Bernard's theory that the liver manufactured sugar,† and that therefore Diabetes may con-

* All Physiologists, whose works I have read, admit that sugar is always met with in the hepatic vein, though none be discovered in the Vena Porta.

† This Physiologist fed a well-nourished adult dog for seven days on sheep's heads, then he killed it, and found sugar in the hepatic vein though there was none in the portal vein.

sist of an exaggerated normal function of the liver. We shall enter further upon this subject when we consider the important question, what constitutes Diabetes or in what does Diabetes consist?

CHAPTER II.

SYMPTOMS.

ATTENTION to the general symptoms of Diabetes is of the greatest importance; and although the presence of sugar in the urine is a symptom essentially characteristic of the disease, yet it is always accompanied with well marked general symptoms. These bear a relation, within certain limits, not to the quantity of sugar excreted by the kidneys, but rather to the quantity retained, mixing itself with, and poisoning, the various organs and tissues of the body; I say within certain limits, because if the quantity of sugar be very large, it must be derived in part from the decomposition of the tissues of the body, and then the symptoms of debility and loss of weight will bear a relation to this excessive drain upon the system, and will accordingly be well pronounced. The first symptoms that attract the notice of patients are thirst, increased secretion of urine, and frequency of micturition.

Thirst.—This is usually great, almost unquenchable. I shall never forget the misery I endured. It is increased generally after taking food; it is greatest in the evening and at night, and it is astonishing how much fluid is often drunk during the night. In my own case three or four tumblers were consumed, though only sufficient was taken at a time to moisten the mouth, and kept long before swallowing it. Anxiety augments it greatly. This is the least exceptional of all the symptoms; I have only met with one case in which it was absent, the other symptoms were strongly marked, the urine having a specific gravity of 1042, amount about 72 ounces in 24 hours, and containing about 10 grains of sugar in the ounce. M. Bouchardat endeavoured to establish a certain relation between the quantity of starch taken as food, and the thirst, viz. as 1 to 7; but this relation was found very different by M. Jordâo in his experiments, being as 1 to 18. The mouth is generally very dry, with often a sweetish taste. The tongue varies, at times natural in colour, at other times dirty, covered with a thick yellowish fur. The saliva is generally scanty, viscid, and acid, in one case, however, and that not a severe one, I found it alkaline.

The *urine* is very abundant, it has a relation to the fluid taken; the greatest quantity is secreted during the night and towards morning. The amount passed in the twenty-four hours is sometimes considerable. "It has exceeded in more than one instance 70 lbs. In the case of Smith, detailed in the Writer's hospital *Facts and Observations*, 36 pints were voided in twenty-four hours, and in that of Johnson 32 pints. The amount is generally less than the liquid ingesta, but it has been found in one or two cases that the amount of urine considerably exceeded the whole amount both of the solid and liquid ingesta. This fact has been satisfactorily established by Dr. Bardsley, who has shewn that the excess of the former cannot be accounted for solely on the supposition of its being derived from a general wasting and diminution of the solids of the body; for in two or three instances, during the period in which the amount of urine passed almost daily exceeded the quantity of fluid contained in the liquids and solids taken, the patient had gained many pounds in weight. The author receives the fact without framing any hypothesis to explain it, though he states that the researches of modern physiologists, particularly those of Klapp and Dangerfield, render it extremely probable that this superabundant quantity of fluid is absorbed by the lungs from the moisture of the atmosphere." (*Art: Diabetes, Cyclopædia of Practical Medicine*, vol. I.) I paid particular attention to this point in my own case, but I always found the fluid taken exceeded the quantity of urine made. The average amount of fluid taken daily for a week, was from 100 to 110 ounces, the quantity of urine from 90 to 95 oz.

When I perspired the quantity of fluid drunk was about the same, but the quantity of urine was reduced to 63—68 oz.* Micturition is painless, but the desire is generally imperative. This with me was most marked. The colour of the urine seems to depend upon the quantity of sugar it contains; when but little, it is scarcely at all changed, but on the contrary, when the amount of sugar is large, the colour is much diminished: as a rule all urine containing much sugar is pale, and of a less marked colour. The colour varies at different hours of the day, having some relation to digestion. The specific gravity depends upon the quantity of sugar and urea it contains; in those who eat largely of animal food the specific gravity is raised considerably, I believe from an excess of urea; in those who eat sparingly the speci-

* I may state that the quantity of urine made varied considerably, depending upon the amount of perspiration.

fic gravity is more in accordance with the sugar contained. The specific gravity of healthy urine may be said to range between 1018 and 1025, being higher in summer than in winter, on account of the increased perspiration; in diabetes it ranges between 1025 and 1056, the latter is the highest I have seen; its usual range is between 1025 and 1042. The odour is very peculiar. Sir Thomas Watson describes it as "more like the faint smell of certain apples or rather of an apple-chamber;" often the smell is like honey or whey. According to M. Rayer, the odour mawkish at the moment of emission becomes alcoholic if left to itself, and undergoes fermentation: if exposed to the air for twenty-four or forty-eight hours it has a well pronounced ammoniacal smell: the odour varies at different times of the day, and is also affected by the treatment employed. The taste is generally sweet, sometimes insipid, and has been found even acid. When allowed to stand the urine becomes peppered over its surface with small scales resembling white wax, or as if small portions of melted wax candle had been dropped on the surface; these specks gradually coalesce into a whitish leathery-looking substance of considerable thickness and toughness, adhering to the sides of the glass; this has been called the diabetic ferment; when well washed and preserved in water it gives no indication of change, but if a solution of sugar be added immediately there is evidence of fermentation. On examining this substance by the microscope it will be found to consist of jointed confervoid growths and ovoid vesicles, isolated or united in little chains.* Chemically, the characteristic, indeed the pathognomonic sign of Diabetes, as far as this secretion is concerned, is the presence of sugar; the amount varies greatly. Bouchardat has found it as much as one seventh of the weight of urine, at other times one thirtieth, or even less. The amount of sugar varies from various causes; the quantity of starchy or saccharine aliment has great influence on its amount. Acute Bronchitis, Pneumonia, febrile attacks, or the application of numerous blisters diminishes it much, or may even cause it to disappear for a time.

Authors have spoken of an insipid sugar, but Bouchardat has shown that this sugar is only a mixture of ordinary starch, lactate of

* Some idea of the severity of the disease may be formed from the time required by this covering to spread itself over the surface; if soon the quantity of sugar is large, if more slowly formed the quantity of sugar is small.

soda, chloride of sodium, and extractive matter; when this sugar exists, according to the same author, it is to be considered as a good sign showing that the disease is on the decline.

The presence of sugar is not the only change in the chemistry of the urine. In those cases where the appetite is very great and much animal food is taken, the quantity of urea may rise from 496 grains (32 grammes),* about the normal quantity, to 1457 grains (94 grammes.) Creatinine is also increased from ·45 grammes or 7 grains, the normal daily excretion, to 8·4 grammes or 128 grains. The Chlorides shew an increase from 170 grains (11 grammes) a day to 558 grains (36 grammes). In cases where great emaciation is taking place I have found a large deposit from adding a solution of Tannin; now it is well known, "whatever the peculiarity of the albuminoid body may be, whether Albumen, Syntonin, Casein, Gluten, Legumen, that it is transformed in the stomach into an almost identical albuminoid; moreover this albuminoid, or as it has been called, peptone, possesses properties which distinguish it from other albuminoids, it is no longer coagulable by heat or by nitric acid, though still coagulable by Tannin, metallic

* Taking the gramme at 15·5 grains.

salts, and strong alcohol."* In some cases I have met with there seems to be not only a want of power to assimilate sugar, but also peptones, hence the rapid emaciation. In all urine there is a deposit on adding Tannin, but when the health is good this is small. This is what we should almost expect, for we find, as Dr. Playfair says, that in the shape of cellulose, starch globules, and muscular fibre, one twelfth of the Nitrogen in the food passes away by the bowels; so I believe in all cases, even in the most healthy subject, some peptone passes away by the kidneys, but in severe cases of Diabetes, where the patient rapidly emaciates, large quantities are discovered in the urine.† This multiplicity of materials eliminated by the kidney seems to prove that in Diabetes the modifications in nutrition are very complex, and that non-assimilation of sugar is not the only evil to be feared.

With increased thirst, increased quantity and change in the urine, there is generally a

* Marshall's *Physiology.*

† I have lately been making experiments on this point, and its relation to sugar and urea, at the College of Chemistry, Great Marlborough-st., and shall publish an account of the results obtained as soon as a sufficient number of cases has been collected.

very dry skin: the skin is dry and harsh even in the warmest weather; this is not, however, a constant symptom even when the quantity of sugar contained in the urine is great. In my own case though the skin was very dry at first, after a short time I perspired freely, the least exertion causing the perspiration to pour down my face; yet the quantity of sugar in an ounce of urine was eight grains, amount of urine in twenty-four hours sixty-eight ounces. The perspiration was remarkable for its acidity, reddening litmus paper almost as deeply as a mineral acid. Sugar has been discovered in the perspiration by McGregor, Auteureith, Semola and others: the latter author reckoned the quantity of sugar excreted by the skin daily equal to twenty milligrammes; the maximum quantity was in the night and morning; the food whether exclusively azotised or starchy made no difference. When the disease is far advanced the skin often becomes rough and scaly; in some cases an eruption of Lichen, Psoriasis, or Impetigo occurs. Sometimes the skin loses its sensibility, hairs may be pulled out without the patient feeling. When the fatal termination approaches profuse perspiration often occurs.

The bowels are generally confined, the fæces

are dry, hard and scybalous, and passed with difficulty: at times they contain fatty matter; is there disease of Pancreas then? The colour is generally that of health: sometimes, especially towards the end, diarrhœa alternates with constipation, becoming gradually more and more continuous so as quickly to exhaust the patient: sometimes the bowels refuse to act and death may result from this. Respiration is often more feeble and frequent than in health. M. Jordâo found the maximum about eighteen per minute. The effect of Diabetes on respiration has been minutely studied by Voit and Pettenkofer: in confirmed Diabetes the quantity of oxygen absorbed is much less than in health, less carbonic acid is also exhaled. The relation is the following, in twenty-four hours.

	Sound man.	Diabetic man.
Oxygen absorbed	708·9	572·2
Carbonic Acid exhaled	911·5	659·3
Water excreted	828·	611.3

Further it is known that in a healthy man by increasing animal food the absorption of oxygen is also increased; in Diabetes this is not the case; the same authors give the following results.

	Sound man.	Diabetic man.
Mixed food	832 oxygen.	680 oxygen.
Animal food	865 „	613 „
Inanition	760 „	340 „

Thus the diabetic has in his blood, so to speak, more combustible matter; as a rule he eats more than a healthy man, he absorbs less oxygen, burns less. The quantity of vapour given off by respiration is also less than in health.

In Diabetes there is often a cough, dry at first, accompanied with short breathing, afterwards expectoration occurs: in the expectoration Bernard and others discovered sugar. Pneumonia or Tubercular disease is often met with; according to Dr. Pavy there is a breaking down of the lung tissue, the result of simple chronic inflammation, and the formation of cavities without being preceded by, or accompanied with, any strumous or tubercular deposits: this state of things is rare at the beginning of the disease, for generally at this period the respiratory murmur is distinct, and percussion indicates nothing wrong: sometimes true Pulmonary Consumption shows itself and rapidly leads to death.

Accompanying Diabetes, and especially when the disease is severe, there is feebleness of limbs; the patient soon becomes fatigued; power diminishes: the muscles become flabby, the patient falling into a state of general atony followed often by quick exhaustion. The voice often becomes weak as the disease advances; the sight enfeebled: amaurosis and cataract are apt to occur. The intellectual faculties are generally clear, though there is listlessness and a sad depressed look. Vague pains are often complained of in the back and loins; at times the feet swell. Sleep is much disturbed by dreams, the mind in some cases seems hardly ever to be at rest. The generative function lessens in power; a time comes when all desire fails; so a return of the desire is a good sign: insupportable itching of the vulva in women at times occurs, at other times erythema of the parts; when such a state of things is met with, an examination for sugar ought always to be made.

In some cases it is remarkable how long the patient will preserve his *embonpoint:* but uniformly towards the termination of the disease the emaciation becomes extreme. Dr. Fonseca of Pernambuco, South America, found boils and carbuncles so frequent as to be regarded as a symptom characteristic of Diabetes. That they are owing to the sugar in the blood is rendered probable from the following case in the practice of M. Lorain. Two confectioners, in order to economize their money, were accustomed to eat as much sugar as they could; after fifteen or eighteen days of this food they were both seized with an eruption of boils, and were considerably emaciated; no sugar was found in the urine.

Jaccoud, *Clinique Medicale*, 1867, says, certain facts observed by Romberg, Girard, Becquerel, and Griesinger have shown the existence of Diabetes in individuals employed in the fabrication of sugar. It appears that the daily consumption of an excess of sugar greatly modifies nutrition. Aliment exclusively saccharine has produced symptoms similar to starvation. Magendie relates the following. An English physician, Dr. Stark, in order to appreciate the nutritive properties of sugar, lived on it entirely for a month, he was then obliged to give up this food: he had become very feeble, his legs were swollen, his face presented livid red spots: he died shortly after. Carbuncles occur sometimes on the nape of the neck, and are very fatal, erysipelas setting in, followed by exhaustion, and death.

The pulse at the beginning is generally normal in frequency and strength but becomes weaker and quicker as the disease advances. In a state of health the serum of the blood, habitually clear, becomes opaline some hours after food, if the food be of a fatty character.

Drs. Rollo, Dobson, and McGregor considered this the natural state in Diabetes; this is proved to be incorrect. Sugar has been found in the blood but never in very large quantities; Dr. Becker found that Glycosuria resulted if the sugar in the blood exceeded 5 decigrammes in 100 grammes. M. Bouchardat endeavoured to procure crystallized sugar from the blood, but did not succeed.

Patients often suffer from cold feet, especially at night. As regards temperature M. Donné and Jordaô have found it vary under the axilla from 35° C. (95° F.) to 36° C. (96·8° F.). I have examined the temperature in several cases and in all, unless near the termination, have found it natural, that is to say about 98° F. varying a few tenths more or less. Finally, whenever a patient presents thirst, parched and dry mouth, and dry skin, with an increase in the quantity of urine and more frequent micturition, and still further if added to these we have loss of flesh and muscular power, an examination of the urine for sugar should be made.

CHAPTER III.

Causes of Diabetes.

In speaking of the causes of Diabetes we must ever remember that they act only in certain conditions of the body, and these conditions are unknown, and will probably ever remain so, until we see such causes act. There is therefore in all cases of Diabetes a something added to the body, not discoverable it is true, which makes causes, that would otherwise be inoperative, produce the disease in question.

Causes may be divided into predisposing and exciting.

I. *Predisposing.* Constitutional predisposition. This has been disputed, but most authors are agreed in attributing much influence to this cause. The following consideration should have some weight in determining the question; there are three elementary principles which serve for the nutrition of the healthy body, Albuminoid, Fatty, and Saccharine or Amylaceous: from a defect of assimilation of the first we have gout or gravel: from a defect in the second we have fat deposited in various parts of the body: and from a defect in the third we have Glycosuria or Diabetes. As the first two are universally allowed to be constitutional or hereditary, so I think ought also the third. Authors describe numbers of cases of Diabetes that appeared in the same family and amongst near relations. I have seen Diabetes in a brother and two sisters, and a cousin, and I think there can be no doubt of its being hereditary. I have been much struck in my patients with the number of their near relations who have been affected with diseases that are allowed to be hereditary; consumption and scrofulous diseases being especially prevalent: one patient, for instance, had a mother die of consumption, a sister of hydrocephalus, a brother from scrofulous knee-joint, another sister from malignant disease of the womb: in another family one brother and two sisters were affected with Diabetes and two or three died of malignant disease. I might say that in eighteen cases where the history was carefully ascertained all had some relations who had died of consumption, or had scrofulous or malignant diseases. M. Mialhe says he has observed the disease in three brothers; in two brothers of another family, and he has often seen a diabetic patient have a brother who was troubled with gravel.

Sex. In the 10 years from 1850 to 1860, 4564 deaths from Diabetes were registered in England

and Wales: 3032 of these were males, 1514 females; the disease being about twice as common in males as in females. It is important to remark that the development and exercise of the sexual functions appear to increase the liability to diabetes in both sexes; and the diminished frequency of the disease in women after 45, as compared with men of the same age corresponds with the earlier de cline of the sexual activity in the female sex: the maximum mortality in males is between 45 and 55, in females between 25 and 35.

Age. Diabetes prevails among young and middle-aged men; the deaths being rare under 5 years of age. I have not seen a case under 8 years, but in the Register of deaths for 1861 9 under 5 years of age are entered, 5 males and 4 females: in 1867, 7 cases are registered, 4 males and 3 females. Dr. Prout has seen only one case in a child 5 years old, and only 12 between the ages of 8 and 20 out of a total number of 700. Dr. West, in the third edition of his work on the *Diseases of Infancy and Childhood*, 1854, says a case has never come under his notice, but in the fifth edition, 1865, he mentions two cases, one a girl 3½ years old and the other, her sister, 2½.

After 65, Diabetes is comparatively rare, judging from the number of deaths that then take place; the mortality is greatest between 25 and 65, and is tolerably uniform between these ages. In extreme old age death from Diabetes is very rare, not only absolutely but as to the mortality from all other causes.

Dr. Bence Jones however considers it more frequent. Of 29 patients 11 were over 60, and of these 6 were over 70. It must however be noted, according to M. Dechambre, that many old people have sugar in their urine which he says is due to imperfection of the colouring matter of the blood.

Occupation. Urban and manufacturing districts suffer more from Diabetes than rural; if we take London, Lancashire, and the West Riding of Yorkshire, as representing the former, we find the mortality from Diabetes as 2·5; 3·2; and 4·1 respectively, for every 100,000 inhabitants; whilst in Wales and the Southern Midland Counties, which are mostly agricultural, the respective numbers are 1·2 and 1.5 for the same number of inhabitants.*

Condition and Temperament. It is most frequently seen in those who appear to be strong and in good condition. In 100 cases in

* Roberts' *Urinary Disease*, p. 165.

which this has been noticed 70 seemingly were strong.

Cowley and Willis considered that the lymphatic temperament predisposed to the disease. Nicolas and Gaudeville considered the muscular most prone. M. Jardaô thinks the lymphatico-nervous the most liable. Of 72 cases I have collected, in which the temperament was mentioned, the following is the relative frequency.

Lymphatic	20.
Nervous	14.
Sanguine	12.
Bilious	12.
Lymphatico-nervous	8.
Nervo-sanguine	6.

Season and Climate. The action of these two is undoubtedly alike, but they must have different results. Seasons have only a fleeting influence, climate produces deep modifications in the constitution. M. Gontour in his treatise gives this short resume of our knowledge, "Diabetes is nowhere more common than in England and Holland. Dr. Willis says that his friend Dr. Babington informed him that, while he was preparing to pass an examination at Cambridge, his father who had an extensive practice shewed him 33 cases of this disease at one time. It is believed that the cold and damp climate is the sole cause of this frequency, but the manner of living of the inhabitants has perhaps a greater influence in the production of the disease than the constitution of the atmosphere; indeed, one sees that Diabetes becomes rarer in cold countries, and occurs more frequently in certain warm ones. Thus Sir Charles Lefevre says he examined the register of the principal Hospitals, civil and military, of the Russian Empire and did not find the mention of a single case. Sir James Wylie did not meet with a single example among more than two millions of soldiers whom, as Inspector General of the Russian army, he had examined. On the other hand, Diabetes is far from being rare in Portugal, Ceylon, St. Dominique, or Egypt; in the latter country the Arabian, Rable Moyses, has seen 20 cases in 10 years and adds "Quod multoties generatur (Diabetes) in regionibus calidis et forte accidit in regione Ægypti saporitate aquæ Nili quam omnes bibunt." P. Frank has met with this disease more frequently in Italy than in Germany; "during 20 years'" says he, "in which I have practised among the different people of Germany I have seen only 3 cases of this disease; in Italy in the short space of 8 years

I have met with 7 cases." In France, Diabetes is common enough. M. Rayer has seen more than 30 cases. "Some particulars which I have collected," says M. Contour, "lead to the belief that Diabetes is more common in Normandy:" this opinion was put forth by Nicolas and Gaudeville who attributed the frequency to the food of the inhabitants and especially to the use of fermented drinks, as for example cider, which is the common beverage."*

Aliments and Drink. The question has been much discussed whether the sugar in Diabetes entirely arises from the aliment, and though it has been decided that it does not altogether come from this source, yet much importance must be attached to food. M. Contour was struck with the great number of diabetic cases that owe their origin to an insufficient reparative diet or an almost exclusively vegetable one. Most of the patients I have seen were great eaters of bread and potatoes.

Drinks, such as beer, cider, perry, &c., have been considered as a cause of Diabetes and this because the disease is more common in England and Holland where the beverages are much used. Majendie mentions, in his *Dictionary of*

* Valleix *Guide de Medicin Practicien*, second edition, vol. iii. p. 555—6.

Medicine and Practical Surgery, that a man who had eaten nothing but potatoes for 15 days was seized with Diabetes. It has been considered that the abuse of condiments, especially of pepper, which are exciting in their nature contributes to this disease. M. Bernard made the following experiment on two dogs: he injected water into the stomach of one, into the stomach of the other he injected Ether; he then killed them; he found but little sugar in the hepatic veins of the first, whilst in the second there was a large proportion. Here the direct effect of a stimulant on the liver is seen. According to M. Bouchardat the greater number of cases are met with in those leading a sedentary life. In France he finds notaries having the sad privilege of being the most subject to this disease. He considers the sugar in these cases to arise from their studious habits, from their want of exercise and from having only time to take one copious meal, or at the most two meals during the 24 hours, swallowing their food quickly without properly masticating it; also being usually rich, they live well. The curates in great cities are also liable to Diabetes, they generally have only one, an abundant repast in the day, and the hours passed in the performance of their duties at the confessional are hours of almost absolute rest.

Medical men are placed next; this disease is met with in the more fortunate members of the profession who live well and take but little exercise. It occurs also to the general practitioner who has a large practice: to save time he is obliged to drive, and being over-fatigued sleeps in his carriage; takes but few meals and eats quickly. M. Bouchardat adds that it is to be met with in all social positions in which there is found great ease of circumstances united with great mental exertion and a sedentary life. He further adds, he is sure he is not wrong in saying that in 20 men between 40 and 60, taken either from the legislative assembly, or from the learned bodies, or from those holding the highest positions in commerce, finance, or even the army, one would be found whose urine contained sugar.

Diabetes is frequently seen in those who have led a very active life, and then suddenly given themselves up to ease and tranquility. An unhealthy moist situation has been considered a cause.

A gentleman, a lawyer in a large way of business, consulted me at Tunbridge Wells: he came from rather a damp locality; he had been gradually losing flesh: he was considerably emaciated; he had little thirst, a bad appetite, and complained of great physical as well as mental exhaustion: he slept badly: his bowels were loose: urine, specific gravity 1040., amount 74 ounces in 24 hours, and contained a considerable amount of sugar. I ordered a grain of opium and the same of sulphate of quinine at bedtime; without further treatment, except going out in the open air and walking as much as he could without fatigue, he improved immediately. In 10 days, the urine was clear of sugar, specific gravity 1022, amount 46 ounces: in 3 weeks he left very much improved having gained several pounds in weight.

The next year he returned with all the old symptoms, and sugar in the urine. In about 14 days it disappeared under the opium and quinine treatment with walking. This time he took the Tunbridge waters with great advantage. He left again in 3 weeks completely free from sugar and comparatively speaking well, having again increased in weight. The next year he returned with all the same symptoms. Though the inactive life he led might have had something to do with the Diabetes, according to M. Bouchardat, yet I cannot but think that in this case locality had to do with the Glycosuria, for the symptoms hardly amounted to Diabetes; each time the patient rapidly recovered more quickly than the treatment warranted.

All causes of debility must be ranged among predisposing causes: the disease often develops itself as a consequence of too great mental exertion, excessive evacuations, venereal excess, or too prolonged lactation; also it arises from repeated hæmorrhages, anæmia, or the puerperal state: here the Diabetes must be regarded as a secondary affection and symptomatic of others.

II. *Efficient causes.* These are, first, affections of the nervous system, as traumatic lesions of the brain and nerves; certain cerebral affections, moral effects, strong emotions, profound sorrow, hard and prolonged study, nervous excitement: also too frequent coitus—venus immodica—and onanism, have been reckoned as causes of Diabetes; in two or three severe cases this last habit has been admitted. Sugar is also found in the urine in certain nervous maladies, as hysteria, epilepsy; even after fits of coughing in hooping-cough Glycosuria has existed; but in these cases the usual symptoms of Diabetes do not occur.

Traumatic lesions and diseases of the brain. Irritation of the pneumogastric nerves or pricking the floor of the fourth ventricle or the olivary bodies, from which the pneumogastric nerves arise, has given origin to sugar in the urine. Cerebral disturbances may also determine Glycosuria, such as arise from falls on the head or neck, but the sugar disappears as the effects of the injury pass away: if, however, disease is set up, as the result of these injuries, in the fourth ventricle or its neighbourhood, then the sugar in the urine may become permanent, and the kidneys, not being able to get rid of the quantity formed, its retention gives rise to the constitutional symptoms, and we have Diabetes.

Professor Grisolle mentions a case of Diabetes following upon disease in the nervous centres. A woman aged fifty-two became hemiplegic and, in less than a year after, Diabetes manifested itself with great intensity. The post-mortem examination in a case of Diabetes which had lasted seven years showed small spots of blood between the layers of the optic thalamus and corpora quadragemina. M. Levrat, in his thesis, mentions a case where, on post-mortem examination, a colloid tumour was found in the fourth ventricle.

Dr. Luys, in a post-mortem of a case of Diabetes, found the anterior wall of the fourth ventricle was more vascular than in the normal state; the large venous trunks were delineated on its surface. On looking more closely, tawny spots were observed disseminated in the upper parts below the superior processes of the cerebellum, also similar spots below the origin of the auditory nerves: these tawny spots were due to fatty degeneration of the nerve cells; in place of presenting regular shapes, fringed prolongations, and circumscribed nuclei, the cells were transformed into an irregular granular mass exclusively constituted by aggregated yellowish granulations more or less closely attached to each other: so complete was the alteration of tissue, that it might be said that the histological elements had reached the last stage of retrograde evolution and had ceased to exist as anatomical individualities. Dr. Luys describes another case in which there was found great vascularity with brownish discoloration of the anterior wall of the fourth ventricle, which was also notably attenuated. Histological examination disclosed a remarkable turgescence of the minute capillaries, and showed that the presence of the yellow patches, in some places tawny and brownish, was solely due to a peculiar degeneration of all the cells of the nervous tissue. The cells in progress of retrograde evolution were filled with yellowish granulations, having jagged, half-destroyed edges and presenting only some scarcely recognisable fragments.*

Dr. Dickinson, also, in the last volume of the *Royal Medical and Chirurgical Society's Transactions*, has described five cases of post-mortem in Diabetes, in which peculiar morbid changes were constantly found in the cerebro-spinal system; in all the alterations were of the same nature, and for the most part in the same situation. The earliest change recognised was a dilatation of the arteries, followed by a degeneration of the nervous matter at certain points external to them. The extension of the degenerative process produced cavities seen without the microscope; these cavities contained blood vessels, extravasated blood, grains of pigment, and the product of nerve decay. These contents were absorbed, simple vacuities being left. These were found in every part of the spinal cord and encephalon, attaining their greatest development in the medulla oblongata and pons varolii.

Sugar has also been met with in affections of the spinal cord. M. Becquerel mentions a case of acute myelitis in which it was found; also a case of spinal meningitis with inflammatory swelling of the pia mater, softening of

* Trousseau's *Clinical Medicine*, Vol. 3, p. 495, etc.

cord substance, and a cyst in the cerebellum. Lebert has seen a hæmorrhage into the upper part of the spinal column accompanied with intense Diabetes. In the works of Scarlau two cases are mentioned, in which there were all the constitutional symptoms of Diabetes and the autopsy showed softening of the cord, hypertrophy of the meninges and gelatinous exudation into them.

Irritation of the pneumo-gastric nerve is a cause. Mr. Nyman,* at the autopsy of a gentleman who had long suffered from Diabetes, found, on examining the thorax, a calculous mass the size of a hazel nut beneath the bifurcation of the trachea which appeared to exercise pressure upon the nerve: he met with the same state three times when making the post-mortem examination on cases of Diabetes: in fact, irritation of any part of the pneumogastric may cause the disease, it being the afferent nerve to the fourth ventricle, from whence the impression is reflected, through the sympathetic, to the liver and so producing Diabetes.

* G. Nyman 1857. *Dublin Hospital Gazette*, Vol. no. 14.

CHAPTER IV.

The General Course of Diabetes.

It usually begins insidiously. It is most frequently recognized by the progressive increase of thirst and of urinary secretion. About the same time the mouth becomes dry, and there are often noticed on the sides of the tongue two streaks of whitish saliva. Before this the patient has sometimes been troubled with dyspeptic symptoms, weight and oppression at the pit of the stomach, acid eructations, disagreeable taste in the mouth, pains in the head, unusual restlessness, pains in the limbs, troublesome dreams, &c. Frequently then, as Dr. Bence Jones has remarked, the disease is arrested for a time, taking a slower, but progressive, course: at times there are seasons of remission—this has been during summer. A true periodicity has been observed; this tendency shewing itself usually in the spring. But this generally terminates by becoming confirmed Diabetes. After a time the symptoms become more permanent and intense; the thirst, and often the appetite, increases; the amount of urine increases; the saliva becomes more viscid; there is no perspiration; the strength diminishes; emaciation progresses; the voice becomes feeble; the power of producing heat diminishes, also the generative function; there is general restlessness; the sleep is much disturbed; vague pains are felt in the head, back, and limbs; there is a feeling of great depression. Often at this time eruptions on the skin and boils manifest themselves. This state of things may go on even for years: then the symptoms become greatly intensified: the thirst becomes excessive; the tongue, dry, red, and often covered with a black fur in the morning; the breath has a sweetish and often a fœtid odour. The digestion becomes more and more troublesome, accompanied with much flatulence, often a perfect disgust for food, vomiting may occur. The tendency to constipation, which before existed, now gives place to diarrhœa. The quantity of urine may diminish much, though the sugar in it remains considerable, or quite at the last may disappear. The skin ceases to act, and at this time carbuncles or even gangrene may be developed. Albumen also may be found in the urine, and the deposit from adding tannin, or a solution of zinc is very great, even when no change takes place by heat and nitric acid. The senses as well as the intellectual powers, now become dull;

the prostration is extreme; the ankles and feet become œdematous; the pulse gradually becomes weaker, and life is slowly extinguished, if there does not occur a complication, which is frequently met with, and carries off the patient more rapidly: the physician leaving the patient in a state not indicating immediate danger; in a short time after death occurs.

Such is the course of the disease when it goes on to a fatal termination; but, happily, in the greater number of cases, the symptoms are ameliorated, and by proper treatment the disease is often cured.

When the disease terminates favourably, the symptoms gradually diminish, the quantity of urine secreted lessens, it recovers its proper colour and smell, acquires its normal specific gravity, and finally the sugar disappears.

The course of Diabetes is greatly modified by the constitution of the individual. The symptoms vary in the order of their developement and appearance. For example, the patient may remain for a long time in good condition, and the function of digestion may be well performed. The sugar sometimes disappears during the course of an eruption, diarrhœa, or an accession of fever. M. Guerand,

Physician to the Hotel-Dieu, knew a Professor of Physiology in whom the disease alternated with gout; the Diabetes was cured by a diet of meat, coffee, &c.; he then put himself on a diet of meat and vegetables to cure the gout.

The course of Diabetes is, at times, very rapid;—at times, very slow. It has, therefore, been divided into Acute and Chronic. The former is very rare. Some authors have spoken of its being fatal in a few days, but the probability in such cases is that it had escaped notice and that complications had promptly arisen. Dobson, however, gives a case where death occurred at the end of five weeks, and Frank one in which the whole course until a fatal termination was only seventy days. Generally the disease lasts for years. Its duration will vary according to the causes which produce it; this is shown to be so in cases depending upon cerebral disease or injuries; in the first the symptoms increase or diminish according as the disease increases or diminishes, in the second it depends upon the severity of the lesion. In these cases the symptoms are strictly subordinate to the causes which give them birth. Diabetes, which depends upon inherent causes or is constitutional, is generally slow in its progress, sometimes lasting 6, 8, or 10 years before proving fatal. The most frequent complication is pulmonary consumption. Dr. Bardsley seemed to regard it as inevitable, so does Dr. Copland, but this is found not to be the case. Other grave complications in the chest are common enough,—such as congestion of the lungs, exudation into the pleura and pericardium, pneumonia. Cerebral congestion often carries off the patient with extreme rapidity. Boils, ulcerations of the legs, and carbuncles are met with; the last is especially dangerous, being frequently followed by erysipelas, which quickly causes death by exhaustion.

Diagnosis.

It is to be remembered that sugar may and does frequently exist in the urine without constituting true Diabetes: this takes places in certain nervous affections: in some cases of dyspnœa: in an attack of asthma (at present I have a patient under my care, whose urine contains a considerable amount of sugar; he tells me he has had it for 8 years; it was discovered accidentally, and he has not had any general symptoms, as thirst, emaciation, great appetite, or increased secretion of urine: he consulted several physicians, at first not believing in the sugar, but they all agreed as to the presence of sugar in the urine; when I examined it, the specific gravity was 1026, amount in 24 hours, 48 ounces, and containing about 4 grains of sugar in the ounce;)* in Bronchitis, especially in elderly persons; often in gout, indeed sugar is so often found that some authors have proposed a "gouty Diabetes." I have found, in a few cases of gout, sugar in the urine, but there were no symptoms characterising Diabetes; it generally passes away very quickly. When sugar is found in gouty cases, colchicum when given, according to some authors, does not seem to produce its usual good effects. In one case of this kind I found that small doses of colchicum did relieve. In all these cases, and in injuries to the brain, the case can only be considered as one of Diabetes when the sugar is found for a long time

* A medical friend told me that he had had for many years under his care a General who had sugar in his urine, the symptoms were not very severe. Whenever the General felt unusually well, a larger quantity of sugar than usual was found in the urine, which so annoyed him that he expressed himself in rather strong terms to the doctor; feeling himself so well he was sure the doctor must be wrong.

and in notable quantity, and attended with the general symptoms, such as thirst, &c.

We must remember here also how easy it is in animals to excite sugar in the urine by irritating the 8th pair of nerves, or by pricking the origin of these nerves in the interior of the cranium; in such cases however the Glycosuria is transitory. Polyuria shews itself often without the presence of sugar in the urine. It is very apt to occur in old men who are weakly and in some chronic maladies; also it has been observed in certain affections of the nervous centres. We know that M. Cl. Bernard, by pricking the floor of the 4th ventricle in the median line, produced not only an increased secretion of urine, but also sugar in it: he could also, by pricking a little higher up, determine often only an increase in the quantity of urine, thus demonstrating, not only cerebral influence in producing Glycosuria and Polyuria, but also how these two diseases may exist separately. This Polyuria used to be called "Diabetes Insipidus," from the quantity of water made (without sugar or taste;) it is distinguished from true Diabetes by the absence of sugar in the urine, by its low specific gravity and pale colour, by the absence of excessive thirst, and dry skin, and no general emaciation.

From Hippuria. The presence of Hippuric acid, or Hippurates is met with in a certain number of cases in which the nutrition is affected: there is great thirst and the urine is abundant, but it contains no sugar and has a lower specific gravity than in health. Sometimes many of the general symptoms of Diabetes accompany those cases in which there is an excess of urea in the urine. A short time ago I saw a young gentleman about 21, his face was pale and thin; he told me he had a voracious appetite, much thirst and greatly increased secretion of urine; he passed it very frequently and was disturbed usually 4 or 5 times during the night; his skin was dry, he said he never perspired, the bowels were confined: on examining the urine, specific gravity 1030, no sugar was found, but on adding nitric acid a copious precipitate of nitrate of urea almost immediately formed: he got perfectly well by substituting vegetables for a large proportion of his meat diet, and by giving alkalies and tonics. In order, therefore, to constitute diabetes not only certain general symptoms, which have been mentioned, must exist, but also sugar. To detect the sugar I generally use Trommer's test or liq. potassæ. To determine its quantity I use the method given by Dr. Pavy: some have a difficulty in making out the point when decoloration has completely taken place, in such cases the fermentation test according to the rules given by Dr. Roberts in his work on *Urinary Diseases* can be relied upon, at all events you can easily tell by it the relative quantity of sugar and whether it is on the increase or decrease, and this is what the Physician requires.

PROGNOSIS.

This was formerly very unfavourable, indeed Nasse said that an individual who found his urine increase largely in quantity and have a sweetish taste and smell ought to make his will. Now it is more favourable; it varies however according to circumstances. If a case is called Diabetes simply from the presence of sugar in the urine without general symptoms existing, it is easily cured, and I am sure many of the so called cases of Diabetes are of this kind. In infants whilst teething, in fits of hooping cough, of asthma, &c. we find the sugar disappear as the cause on which it depends disappears. The sugar resulting from disturbance, injury, or other alteration of the nervous system is dangerous in relation to the cause. When the Diabetes has not existed long, when the sugar disappears quickly from the urine and with this disappearance the general symptoms improve in an equal ratio, we may augur favourably: on the contrary if the affection be of old date, when the symptoms have been very pronounced and the sugar is abundant, though we may have a great amelioration of the symptoms, we must be cautious in our prognosis, as relapses in such cases are very frequent, and complications are apt to occur and carry off the patient unexpectedly. The disappearance of the sugar, without a corresponding amelioration of the general symptoms, is by no means a sign of improvement even in recent cases, much less in cases of long standing: indeed the disappearance of the sugar is often a sign of a grave complication. The appearance of albumen in the urine is a very dangerous symptom; indicating probably a congestive state of the kidney, commencing organic alteration of their structure from excessive work: M. Rayer considered it a sign that dropsy is threatened. I have only seen three cases of this kind, but dropsy did not follow. Age has a grave influence on our prognosis. Infants and young adults, if the disease is severe, for the most part, die rapidly: in elderly people, that is to say above the age of 45, the prognosis is more favourable, more especially if they are in easy circumstances. M. Bouchardat considered that when there was no tubercle in the lungs, the female had a better chance of recovery than the male. As the patient generally dies from exhaustion, unless some accidental complication occurs, we must regard loss of weight and power with great anxiety; and a dry cough followed by expectoration, with dulness on percussion of the upper part of the chest and morning perspirations, as fatal symptoms. In cases where complications occur we must be very careful in our prognosis, however slight the symptoms may be, as patients often very suddenly and unexpectedly sink.

Finally, in estimating the danger of Diabetes, it is not entirely the quantity of sugar contained in the urine which must guide us, but the quantity retained in the system, which we can discover by an examination of the assemblage of symptoms. We must examine the muscular strength, the state of the skin, the digestive functions, respiration, calorification, the nervous system; we must ascertain also the weight of the patient and see if he is gaining or losing flesh, and the amount of deposit from tannin or solution of sulphate of zinc.

By a due consideration of all these symptoms, together with the quantity of sugar in the urine, shall we alone be able to come to a right prognosis of the disease.

CHAPTER V.

THE NATURE OF DIABETES.

We come now to the important question: What is Diabetes? or in what does Diabetes consist? It was formerly thought that the office of the liver was only to secrete bile, and then it was difficult to explain its size and characters, more especially in the embryo state; but since its influence in the process of sanguification, and especially its Glycogenitic functions have been discovered, its prominence among the glandular organs (to use the words of Mr. Marshall in his work on *Physiology*) can be sufficiently accounted for. Besides its influence in the process of sanguification and in secreting bile, later researches have proved that it has two other important functions to perform.

1st. The formation of Glycogenitic or amyloid matter. This matter seems to be formed not only from the saccharine and starchy substances taken as food, but also at the expense of the nitrogenised substance of the tissues and organs of the body itself: part of this matter in a healthy subject is being constantly carried off by the hepatic veins and assimilated, while the surplus is stored up for future use. It is allowed by all physiologists that this matter is formed in the liver, not only of animals that feed on sugar and starchy matter but also of those that feed exclusively on flesh. That it is largely formed from the saccharine and amylaceous food is clearly proved by the experiments made by Dr. McDonnell, related in his treatise on the function of the liver,* he says it is surprising, almost incredible, to what a degree and with what rapidity the liver may be increased or diminished in bulk by the administration of particular kinds of food.

So far as this is due to an increased or diminished quantity of amyloid substance stored up in the liver the following table will show :—

	Diet consisting almost exclusively of starch and sugar.	On a diet of fat.	On a diet of Gluten bread.	On a diet of Gelatine.
Dogs	980 grs.	Hardly a trace.	125 grs.	None.
Rats	7 „	do.	3 „	do.
Pigeons	25½ „	do.	1 „	do.
Rabbits	45 „	do.	8½ „	do.

Dr. Pavy's experiments corroborate this.

From the above table it is clearly seen how much the amyloid matter is dependent on diet; starch and sugar being the great producers of it.

2nd. The liver, from the amyloid or glycogenic matter, forms an easily assimilated sugar; this

* Dublin, 1865.

in the healthy state is absorbed by the system, so that the amyloid or glycogenitic matter is the intervening stage between the sugar and starch taken as food and the sugar that is to be absorbed by the system in a healthy state. How easily this sugar, compared with other sugars, is assimilated, is shewn by some experiments of Cl. Bernard. He injected under the skin of a rabbit a little more than 7 grains of cane sugar in about one ounce of water, and found decided indications of sugar in the urine: under the same conditions he found he could inject nearly 7 grains of milk sugar, 14½ grains of glucon, 21½ grains of diabetic sugar, and nearly 33 grains of liver sugar, without finding sugar in the urine; hence we see the reason of the re-conversion of the amyloid or glycogenitic matter into sugar. No one can doubt this function of the liver after reading the carefully conducted experiments of Dr. Flint.

In many cases of Diabetes the sugar in the urine cannot have its origin from the sugar and starch taken as food; for it has occurred when the patient has been absolutely restricted to an animal and fatty diet. Observations made with the greatest care by the Rev. S. Haughton *on the phenomena of Diabetes Mellitus*, Dublin, 1861, shew that sugar excreted in

Diabetes has a double origin, being partly derived from the starch and sugar in the food, and partly from the decomposition of protein substances. He considers that the protein compounds resolve themselves into glucose and urea.

This decomposition probably takes place in health also, as in healthy lymph sugar and urea are always found:* the difference being that in health they are given out as the result of work, whilst in Diabetes without work.

Here I may state the difference I make between Glycosuria and Diabetes: in the former there is sugar in the urine, but unattended by very pronounced general symptoms, such as thirst, very dry skin, great emaciation; in fact the general symptoms are so little complained of that the sugar is very often discovered accidently; whilst in Diabetes the sugar in the urine is always accompanied by well marked general symptoms. In the first, the sugar seems to be entirely excreted from the system; whilst in the second, the sugar is retained, and, accumulating in the system, poisons the various tissues and organs, and thus, in proportion to its retention and accumulation, causes danger. Therefore, not Glycosuria only, but also Diabetes may have

* Flint's *Physiology of Man.*

a two-fold origin. 1st. The sugar and starch taken as food, not being converted into amyloid matter, passes through the liver into the general circulation and is excreted by the kidneys as sugar; for De Becker has found that if sugar exists in the blood beyond 5 decigrammes in 100 grammes, (the decigramme being equal to about 1½ grains, therefore about 7½ grains in 1550 grains), Glycosuria must necessarily occur, and it must be got rid of by the kidneys. This non-conversion of sugar into amyloid matter seems to have some relation to the rapidity with which starchy matter is converted into sugar; if a too rapid conversion takes place, it, as it were, overtasks the powers of the liver to convert it into amyloid matter (the power of the liver seems to be limited in this respect); the sugar thus passes through the liver and appears in the kidneys. This fact is, I think, proved from the experiments of M. Bouchardat. He gave 4 dogs and 3 rabbits, a mess of starch, having previously mixed it with diastase: in 5 out of 7 he found sugar in the urine. He adds, that he analysed the urine of these animals after starch had been given without diastase; not the least trace of sugar was found. This experiment seems to prove, also, that the power of the liver to convert starch into amyloid matter varies in animals of the same species. It seems also, from the experiments of M. Lecomte, that for cane sugar to be assimilated it must pass through the liver. If a solution of cane sugar be injected into the jugular vein, the sugar appears in the urine; but if the solution be injected into the vena porta, and so passes through the liver, no sugar appears in the urine.

2nd. Glycosuria and Diabetes may arise from an increased production of sugar, beyond what the powers of the system can assimilate, the surplus being carried off by the kidneys.

The first defect, the sugar not being converted into amyloid matter, may arise in four ways. 1. In the liver itself, from diminished powers in the nerves that supply it. 2. From a large portion of the structure of the liver being destroyed by disease. 3. From a deficiency in the powers of the nerves that supply the stomach, upper part of the intestines and pancreas. 4. From disease in those parts so that their structure is altered; especially is this the case in diseased pancreas, thus preventing the sugar from being duly elaborated for its conversion into amyloid matter.

In 1864 I was consulted at Tunbridge Wells by a gentleman who was labouring under Diabetes; he had read Claude Bernard's theory about the sugar-forming power of the liver: he considered Diabetes as the result of an excessive formation of sugar. On this supposition he had abstained rigidly from all stimulants and had adopted a moderately restricted diet; he ate ordinary bread but well toasted; he eschewed potatoes, sugar, rice, and all fruits. I prescribed iron, ammonia, a table-spoonful of brandy in cold water for luncheon and dinner, and one glass of Ammontillado sherry after. The effect astonished him, for before I saw him he had been losing weight, his thirst was great, and he complained of great muscular debility. He was making about ninety-five ounces of urine a day, specific gravity 1042, it contained a considerable quantity of sugar; he was generally disturbed four times during the night. A week of the above treatment reduced the water to seventy-five ounces, specific gravity 1032, sugar much diminished. This was the first case in which I saw there was a Diabetes from loss of power; in fact the good or bad results of the stimulant plan of treatment is the best test as to whether the Diabetes depends upon an increased formation of sugar in the liver, or upon a defective power of the liver to form glycogenitic or amyloid matter. In another case I lately saw, the benefit arising from the use of ammonia and alcohol in some form was most marked. Under the treatment the patient was gradually improving; from some whim he discontinued it, he became worse, began to lose flesh, to become depressed in spirits, to make more water and pass it more frequently: on recommencing to take the ammonia and alcohol and iron he again improved. Here the good seemed to me to result from stimulating the liver to form the amyloid or glycogenitic matter.

2. When the structure of the liver is almost destroyed by atrophy or by fatty degeneration of its structure, sugar is often detected in the urine: here it does not seem possible from increased action of the liver. In a case of atrophy which I saw some time ago, a considerable quantity of sugar was detected in the urine, and on post-mortem examination the liver was so small as to weigh 35 ounces instead of 50 or 60, the normal weight: the organ was pale, the vessels and ducts in the portal fissure passing through a quantity of firm fibrous tissue.

3. The diminished nervous influence seems to manifest itself in the nerves that supply the mouth, stomach, pancreas and upper part of the

intestines. In such a case there is usually great acidity, the patient being plagued with burning pains in the stomach, sour eructations, the salava in some cases is secreted acid as shown by litmus paper, &c. In this case, the sugar and starch taken as food do not seem to be sufficiently elaborated to be changed into amyloid or glycogenitic matter. This cause of Diabetes, I believe, is seen in those cases where benefit is so strikingly manifested from neutralizing the acidity by alkalies. Here we may have an explanation of the great benefit derived from them, not as Miahle thought, from the blood being too acid, or not sufficiently alkaline, for this has been proved not to be the case, but from the materials introduced into the blood from the digestive organs not being sufficiently elaborated from excessive acidity, and therefore incapable of undergoing the upward change necessary for being utilized by the system, namely by being changed into amyloid matter.

4. Excessive acidity may arise from disease of the pancreas. Cases of Glycosuria and Diabetes are related by Dr. Bright, in which the head of the pancreas formed with the surrounding glands a hard globular mass, and in which the pancreas was hard and cartilaginous. Dr.

Elliotson also relates a case in which the pancreatic duct and large lateral branches were crammed with white calculi. Drs. Marston and Bouchardat record a case in which the pancreas was so degenerated as to be unable to perform its function. In all these cases sugar existed in the urine. Dr. Hyde Salter found the pancreas degenerated in four successive cases of Diabetes, so that he thought he had discovered its true pathology. In all these cases, it seems, from the acidity, that the saccharine matter was not converted into amyloid matter, and thus passing through the liver was excreted as a foreign body. In Dr. Marston's case, there was simply Glycosuria; there were no symptoms leading to the suspicion of sugar in the urine, which was discovered accidentally by chemical examination. Of course in these cases there existed a peculiar predisposition which made causes, otherwise inoperative, act.

The 2nd cause of Diabetes is the increased physiological function of the liver, by which more sugar is formed than can be disposed of. That this is a cause of Diabetes and Glycosuria is proved by post-mortem examination. A case is related by Trousseau in his *Clinical Medicine*, vol. iii. p. 502, in which "the liver was found twice its natural size, the entire surface of the organ was of a uniform greyish colour, substance dense and so resisting as to prevent penetration by the finger; it creaked under the scalpel, the section granular instead of being smooth; there was well-marked cirrhosis, the cirrhosis was hypertrophic. The morbid change did not involve the fibrous so much as the secreting tissue. The fibrous capsule and the trabeculæ which segment the liver were increased in thickness; there was a still more decided augmentation of the volume of the acini, which were visible, projecting from the surface, and also visible on the surface of the section to which they gave a granular character. Thus there was hypertrophy of the liver consequent upon excessive functional activity, hypertrophy especially involving the secreting tissue of the organ. This was evident upon microscopic examination by the aid of which one could see that the hepatic cells, so far from being destroyed or atrophied, were increased in volume and in number."

Frerich in his book, on *Diseases of the Liver*, vol. ii. p. 210, says, there are certain forms of Diabetes in which the anatomical lesion consists in hypertrophy or increased formation of hepatic cells, and he gives two cases in which he examined the liver; in one the organ was considerably enlarged, its form was normal, the outer surface smooth, parenchyma much congested, of a uniform brownish red colour, without distinct indications of lobules, its consistence dense and firm; cells intimately adherent and uniformly pale, form rounded, size small, all contained large shining nuclei, in addition to the cells numerous rounded nuclei with nucleoli were observed, also young cells. In the other case, in addition to young cells and nuclei, some of the hepatic cells were enlarged, while others were of normal character. The hypertrophy of the gland was less remarkable. He adds: Stockvis has carefully traced the appearances indicative of an accelerated cell growth (large cells some of which contained several nuclei, young cells, and free nuclei) in the moderately enlarged liver of a female, aged 30, who died of Diabetes. An increased volume of the liver has been repeatedly met with: Andral's 5 cases and others; but the minute structure of the gland has not been examined. Griesinger observes, that this abnormal state of the liver is by no means a frequent accompaniment of Diabetes; out of 64 cases collected by him there was considerable enlargement of the liver only in 3 and a moderate enlargement in 10. This circumstance, Frerich adds, does not detract from the value of the cases, where enlargement has been proved to exist; increase of cells but serves to show that there are differences in the causes of Diabetes.

The increased physiological function of the liver may be also brought about by the three following conditions. 1. The blood being so stimulating as to excite an increased formation of sugar. 2. From nervous irritation applied directly to the liver. 3. By irritation of nerves, at a distance from the liver.

The first is shewn by the fact that alcohol and other stimulants produce sugar in the urine; this Dr. Harley shewed who injected into the vena porta of several dogs alcohol, ether, liq. ammonia, the dogs immediately became Glycosuric. M. Claude Bernard introduced alcohol into the small intestine of a dog, an abundant Glycosuria was produced. Dr. Harley shewed, in his own case, that stimulating food will produce Glycosuria, which continued some days after the food was discontinued (Harley *on Diabetes*, p. 47, 48).

The second, from irritation applied directly to the liver. Claude Bernard mentions a case in which after a kick from a horse in the region of the liver the patient had Glycosuria until he had recovered from the injury; this might have been converted into Diabetes if the predisposition had existed. I have lately heard of a case where a gentleman fell downstairs striking his right side on the banister: he had great pain in the region of the liver. The next day sugar was detected in the urine by Trömmer's Test: he recovered, and after a few days sugar had completely disappeared.

The third, from irritation affecting nerves at a distance. This influence was first proved by Cl. Bernard's famous experiment in which he produced Glycosuria by pricking the floor of the 4th ventricle. This experiment has been repeated by many physiologists and with the same result. According to Schiff, there seem to be two kinds of Diabetes having a nervous origin; one which he calls "Irritative Glycosuria" exemplified by pricking the 4th ventricle; this form is characterised by its fleeting character, continuing only for some hours or a day; being subject to the general law that irritant action is rapidly exhausted. The other kind he calls "Paralytic Glycosuria;" he illustrates this form by dividing the anterior columns of the spinal cord; the section ought to be made at a point corresponding to the 4th cervical vertebra, or nearer the medulla oblongata. The vessels of the liver become distended, engorged with blood, hyperæmic, and the animal becomes Glycosuric. This form, he says, may continue not only days but weeks, and he considers that this is the form of Glycosuria which is usually met with in practice and proves so rebellious under treatment. It has also been proved that Glycosuria may result from many affections of the nervous centres; whether it is permanent or transitory depends upon the permanent or transitory character of the cause.

From the above view of Diabetes it is evident that it may arise from two great causes: 1st. An exaggerated natural sugar formation of the liver. 2nd. A want of power to convert sugar and amylaceous matter into amyloid substance.

The question naturally arises how are these two conditions diagnosed.

I have generally found that the first condition exists in those cases where the appetite is voracious, where the patient is in, comparatively speaking, a good condition as to flesh, the muscular power considerable, the pulse tolerably strong and not as a rule increased in frequency. On the contrary, in the second case the appetite is generally very small, often absent, indeed there is sometimes an actual disgust for food, the pulse is weak and quick, the condition of the patient as to flesh and muscular power is bad; indeed, I should have affirmed the above distinction absolute, had I not met with a case which presented the latter symptoms, which did not improve with stimulants, but did on their withdrawal. The great distinguishing mark therefore is the effect of treatment; in the former case stimulants are badly borne, in the latter they do good. I was led to form this distinction from considering my own case; for a time I left off all stimulants. I occasionally visited an uncle who was famous for his sherry; I noticed, when I dined there and took three or four glasses of wine, that I had always good nights and, what was then extraordinary to me, the urine passed at bedtime (dining at 5 o'clock) was of a very low specific gravity (1005.) I was not at all disturbed at night on these occasions. After this had happened three or four times I reconsidered my case, took wine and stimulants and from that time greatly improved; in fact with a bath only once a week (though I sponged myself daily); with walking exercise and warm clothing, I got clear of all Diabetic symptoms: no thirst, little increase of urine, 72 ozs. a day, sp. gr. varies from 1036—1040, rarely disturbed more than once in a night;

sugar however still continued in the urine about 6 grains in the ounce, until I conjoined with the above treatment, iron and chlorate of potash, when, after four months, sugar had quite disappeared.

CHAPTER VI.

TREATMENT.

BEFORE proceeding to treatment, I shall give a short account of the difference that exists between the condition of a diabetic and a sound man, taken from M. Gætgcens; the diabetic was his patient and lived with him. The experiment was carried on upon a series of aliments; both took 1500 grammes of meat a day.

	Diabetic.	Sound man.
Urine	3464 grammes.	2318 grammes.
Excrements	227 „	96 „
Sugar	271 „	Traces.
Urea	68 „	52 „
Chloride of Sodium	15 „	10 „

In spite of the great quantity of meat taken, the diabetic did not appease his appetite; while the doctor took as much nourishment as he could, improved upon his diet and gained 45 grammes, the diabetic lost in 4 days 253 grammes: the temperature of the diabetic did not exceed 36·3° C. (98·24° F.) whilst that of the sound man was 37·15° C. (98·87° F.)

Let us now consider shortly the conditions

of life in the diabetic. In him all the functions of the body are altered, secretion, respiration and digestion. There is a large increase of urine; besides the presence of sugar its usual constituents are altered; the quantity of urea as well as creatinine is increased; the salts, especially chloride of sodium, are more abundant: the skin for the most part does not perform its functions. In respiration the quantity of oxygen consumed is far less than in health, also the quantity of carbonic acid given off is diminished. In digestion the albuminous substances are decomposed; according to Griesinger two-fifths of the food taken is converted into sugar; and the number of red corpuscles in the blood is much diminished.

Such being the case the treatment must be, as far as possible, restorative to make up for the immense waste that is taking place. Tranquility of mind is most essential; then every thing that exhausts the system, artificial excitement and stimuli of all kinds are to be avoided. The place of residence should be dry and airy. Sheltered from cold winds, the sleeping room should be large and lofty and exposed if possible to the morning sun.

In the general treatment there are certain points to be strictly attended to.

1st. The diet. This has always been regarded as a subject of the greatest importance. The ancients, as mentioned in the chapter on the history of Diabetes, knew nothing of the pathology of the disease, they had no notion of its connection with sugar in the urine, they considered it as a mere consumption attended with a large discharge of urine, and their treatment was directed to the cure of the wasting and the restraining of the immoderate flow of urine. In Hippocrates' Works the disease is not mentioned under the name of Diabetes, though, in the third book of his Epidemics,* he mentions that "in some cases the urine was not in proportion to the drink administered, but greatly in excess; and the badness of the urine was great, for it had not the proper thickness nor concoction nor purged properly; for in many cases purgings by the bladder indicated favourably, but in the greatest number they indicated a melting of the body, disorder of the bowels, pain and a want of crisis."† Aretæus‡ recommends milk

* Sydenham Society's edition, p. 404.

† Dr. Adams the translator says, "It will readily be understood that a colliquative Diabetes would prove a very unfavourable complication.

‡ Sydenham Society's *Works*, p. 486.

and with it cereals, starch, gruel etc. Paulus Ægineta* recommends more food to be given, and that difficult of digestion and not humid. Sydenham† recommends that the diet be digestible meats, such as veal, wether mutton, &c., no vegetables and no fruit; in fact, he seemed, so far as food was concerned, to have based his treatment on the same principles that were afterwards so strongly insisted upon by Dr. Rollo in this country, and M. Bouchardat in France. Such a restriction of diet is generally used in this country. Dr. Owen Rees, however, has lately opposed this restriction of diet; he says he has no faith in it; he considers that patients do better on a natural diet, i. e. one containing saccharine and amylaceous substances, which, he says, is as necessary as in health, and that abstinence from such food is positively injurious; the circulation of the sugar in the blood producing no bad symptoms: he adds, "I have now had long experience, and am resolved never to countenance a restricted diet." The letters written in answer seem to show clearly how the restricted or animal diet chiefly prevails in this country. There is no doubt that cases do occur occasionally, where diet seems to have

* Sydenham Society, vol, i, p. 547.

† Sydenham Society, vol. ii. p. 17.

no effect on the symptoms and feelings of the patient. I have met with one patient, lately, in whom this was the case. There was no increase of thirst, no increase in frequency of micturition, no discomfort was felt on taking sugar and starchy matter, but there was an increase in the specific gravity of the urine as well as in the quantity of sugar contained in it. On examining it after he had partaken of a meal in which bread, sugar, and amylaceous matter formed a fair proportion, I found the specific gravity was 1035, sugar about 10 grains to the ounce; after a few days' abstinence from sugar &c., the specific gravity was 1030, sugar about 6 grains to the ounce. The general symptoms were not increased, the patient feeling no discomfort in any respect. I believe the following is the explanation of these cases: so long as the excretory organs can free the system of the sugar, no injurious effects are produced and no uncomfortable feelings arise, but if these organs fail to do their duty, the sugar accumulates in the blood, a gradual poisoning of the tissues takes place, and then there are the pronounced general symptoms of Diabetes: but though there is great benefit from a restriction of sugar &c., yet it should be carried out cautiously and slowly. Trousseau says that a diet consisting chiefly of animal food is the most appropriate. The regimen, he adds, ought to contain a certain quantity of herbaceous vegetables which are much more easily digested than feculent substances. I also allow, he further adds, red fruits. If not obtainable other fruits may be eaten, as pears, apples, and even grapes, though they contain a certain quantity of glucose.

Practically, so far as sugar and starchy substances are concerned, there are three types of Diabetes. In the first, by the total suppression of these substances, all sugar disappears from the urine, and this state of things generally continues so long as the diet is restricted. In the second, the sugar is only diminished and this diminution is often temporary. In the third no effect is produced. I should consider the first therefore as the commencement of the disease and of a mild character. Dr. Camplin's case seems to me to have been of this class. I have seen only one case of this kind; the general symptoms were not severe, and the quantity of sugar was not great: after a week on restricted diet, that is to say, meat, eggs, Camplin's flour, milk, toasted brown bread, butter, and iron, the symptoms were greatly improved, and in a month the patient's urine was free from sugar; all thirst was gone and the cure appeared complete. The patient lived four years after, during which time I had an opportunity of seeing him twice; the last time, a year before he died, his urine was free from sugar and he had no symptoms of Diabetes; he died of gastric fever.

In the second type, the sugar found in the urine is evidently furnished either from the azotized substances taken as food or from the patient's tissues. M. Griesinger* made the following experiment in a case where no benefit resulted, as far as the sugar in the urine was concerned, from the withdrawal of all starch and sugar as food: he fed the patient for four days upon an exclusively nitrogenized diet, giving sufficient fluid to appease the thirst. The relation between the weight of food taken and the sugar eliminated was 4320 grammes and 542·32 grammes; by subtracting from the weight of the food taken 70 per cent. for water enclosed in it, the patient took 1296 grammes of extract of meat; the weight of sugar eliminated was a little more than two-fifths of the weight of solid material. According to Schmidt, fresh

* *Studien über Diabeten.* Archiv. für Physiolog. Heilkunde, 1859.

meat contains a mean of 22 per cent. of anhydrous albuminates, consequently the patient received in the 4320 grammes of meat about 950 grammes of anhydrous albuminates; the weight of the sugar was about three-fifths of the aliment: on varying the quantity of animal food taken, it was found that the quantity of sugar was precisely three-fifths of the anhydrous albuminates. Reflecting on the result of these experiments, I have considered it injurious to put patients on an absolute meat diet for a long time, and so force them to make the sugar entirely from the nitrogenized aliment.

My experience is decidedly in favour of a restriction of diet, but very gradually and cautiously carried out. The majority of patients in my practice have been, as stated before, great sugar and starch eaters, being exceedingly fond, and vast consumers, of bread, potatoes, sugar, and fruit. To cut off these articles of diet suddenly, as is often done, I consider injurious; in preparing for a prize fight, where there is present no known disease in the individual training, how slowly and cautiously the restricted diet is proceeded with; we ought surely to proceed at least as cautiously and carefully when we have a defective constitution to deal with. I was a great lover and eater of bread, potatoes, and sweets of every description, and, comparatively speaking, a very small meat eater, taking animal food as a rule only once a day, at dinner, and a small mutton chop satisfied me. On the discovery of my disease, my opinion being that Diabetes was dependent on an exaggeration of the sugar-forming function of the liver, I left off immediately all saccharine and starchy food, adopting a diet as free as possible from these, the only vegetables I allowed myself were spinach, lettuce, asparagus, and cabbage; I took puddings made of Dr. Camplin's flour and the cakes, as purchased of Mr. Blatchley, 362, Oxford Street, London; these I ate with plenty of butter. I combined with this diet the soda bath, walking much, having recognised the advantages of this before reading M. Bouchardat's work, and wearing very warm clothing. Under this treatment I soon began to improve, how much was owing to the diet it is of course impossible to say. It was after my return from Vichy the second time that I determined to relax my diet cautiously, as I found my loathing to the restricted diet became very great: I looked forward to my meals with horror, the very look of cabbage and green food was detestable, my appetite almost failed me; necessity, as it were, compelled me to alter my diet. I then, for the first time, began to use common wheat meal made into bread and cakes; no yeast was used, but it was raised by a powder consisting of tartaric acid one part and carbonate of soda two parts, and this renders the bread alkaline; occasionally also I partook of white bread, having it toasted and eaten cold with plenty of butter: I then added potatoes to my diet, but not eating largely of them. To my astonishment I found myself not only no worse from such a diet, but on the contrary I was becoming gradually stronger; I thoroughly enjoyed my food, and looked forward with pleasure to my meals, and though I still had sugar in the urine, yet it was in somewhat diminished quantity, I had no symptoms which are considered as characteristic of Diabetes; I was generally disturbed only once at night, my thirst was gone, I perspired freely, and instead of losing weight and power, was gradually increasing in both. Quantity of urine, 72 to 79 ounces; sp. gr. 1036 to 1040; in fact the kidneys were able to excrete all the sugar formed, so that there was no accumulation of it in the system. I had Glycosuria but no Diabetes, and it was in my own case that I first began to have a glimmering of the distinction between these two diseases.

In relaxing my diet I used great caution and always employed three tests, which I found soon told me of any error of diet which I had committed, and thereby enabled me to retrace my steps. The 1st, which I consider also the most delicate and decided, was increased dryness of mouth, especially during the night, with slightly increased depression of spirits. 2nd. The increased colour of the urine on boiling with liq. potassæ, with increased quantity, and increased frequency of micturition. 3rd. Weight.* I weighed myself regularly every month. If I increased in weight, or even remained the same, I was satisfied. If the first and third test were right, I did not regard the increased darkening of the urine when boiled with liq. potassæ a reason for giving up a well-considered relaxation of diet, unless it continued for some days. Emboldened by my success I have gradually and cautiously relaxed my diet; always however paying great attention to other means pointed out, especially walking exercise; at this time

* With this we may conjoin the Tannin test, the deposit from which increases, I may say always, with the loss of weight, not having as yet met with a single case in which it has not been so.

I was not aware of the benefit derivable from the long-continued use of small doses of iron, and chlorate of potash, which I have now taken regularly for the last 6 months and have been free from sugar for some time.

My present diet is:

Breakfast. Bacon well done, fish or eggs, brown bread or cakes eaten with plenty of good fresh butter, at times ordinary bread well toasted.

Luncheon. Eggs or soup with maccaroni, or rice, or cold meat, with a table spoonful of brandy or two glasses of claret in a tumbler of water.

Dinner. Soup or fish, meat, green vegetables, potatoes (sparingly), cheese, at times pale ale and a little dry fruit.

I occasionally take two or three glasses of champagne during dinner and never have an appearance of sugar, or any increase in frequency of making water or in the quantity: indeed I always feel the better after taking it. I consider that it is owing to the continued and regular exercise I take that I have been able to relax my diet to this degree; if I take less exercise, which I have occasionally done, I do not feel so well in myself, and feel confident that even now if I were to leave off regular exercise I should soon have to again restrict my diet.

When I am the first to discover the disease in a patient and the symptoms are not severe, and have not existed for a long time, if the diet has consisted of much saccharine and amylaceous food, I commence by cutting off one half of these kinds of food. After four or five days if I find there is an improvement I cut down one half of the remainder. I then wait a few days more, and if there is still improvement I cut off all sugar, potatoes &c. and ordinary bread, giving the patient instead bread made of wheat meal. After a few days I put him on a more stringent diet, giving cakes made after Dr. Camplin's direction or Dr. Pavy's almond bread, meat, and vegetables, such as cabbage, asparagus, lettuce, spinach, &c., which contain no sugar or starchy matter.

This I do, hoping that the case may be found to belong to the first class mentioned above, viz., that in which the sugar depends on the saccharine and amylaceous food taken.

I have found however that with one exception all the cases that I have seen come under the second class, those in which the sugar is only diminished.

When the least loathing for food occurs I immediately relax the stringency of the diet, knowing from experience what courage is required to persevere in it. In general, if such a diet is attempted to be continued, I find the patient, unknown to his physician, breaks through it, and thus that confidence which should exist between physician and patient is lost, and the result cannot be otherwise than injurious. Even if the patient should have the courage to continue such a diet I am sure it would be injurious.

Andral relates the following of a woman who, under the full persuasion that she would be cured by a diet strictly animal, took animal food for two months without the slightest deviation; during this time she took nothing but roast and boiled meat, drinking water to which was added a small quantity of brandy. At the end of this time she abandoned the diet which had become insupportable. When she commenced the animal diet, she was passing 27 grammes of sugar, (about 418 grains) in every litre, (34 ounces) when she left it off, the quantity of sugar was 49 grammes (about 759 grains) in the litre. What is important in this case is this, when she relaxed the diet and took meat, eggs, milk, a little ordinary bread, vegetables, and replaced the alcohol by wine and water, the quantity of sugar began to diminish and there were found 30 grammes, then 26 grammes, and then 15 grammes: however, at the end of some days the sugar, though the same diet was continued, began again to increase and after three weeks the quantity was 54 grammes (about 840 grains) per litre. M. Andral mentions the remarkable fact that he has found in all cases where the diet is suddenly changed, whether the starchy element is taken away and replaced by meat or the converse, that the sugar always diminishes, but that after a time if the same diet is continued the sugar again increases.

This I cannot say is according to my experience, but I attribute it to the other means I employ with the diet. When I relax the diet I do so thus: I first substitute brown bread and cakes for Dr. Camplin's cakes, &c., carefully observing the effect as regards the patient's feelings and testing the water as above stated; then I relax a little more, allowing first one thing, then another, until the patient's diet becomes like my own, as mentioned above: if any increase of symptoms occur, which I must say is not often, proceeding in this cautious way, I immediately retrace my steps, cutting off the last food that seems to have been the cause of the increase, and then remaining quiet for a week or two before permitting any further relaxation.

In those cases where the Diabetes has existed a long time and consequently has been under a variety of treatment, I never use the absolutely restricted diet, as I am sure they belong to the second class of cases. I begin by putting them on the wheat meal bread and am guided in other matters of diet by the patient's history, till I gain experience for myself in the case.

Milk I find can be taken for the most part without harm, and when there is a great love for it, which is often the case, I always allow it. Animal sugar is much more easily digested than vegetable; when it produces indigestion, as it sometimes does, a little lime water added to it will often cause it to be borne well. In those cases where great debility exists, two thirds of a tumbler full of milk and one third lime water, with a dessert or table spoonful of brandy taken early in the morning has been of great benefit.

I have only tried in two cases a milk diet as recommended by Dr. Smart of Edinburgh, who asserted that during the time it was taken the sugar disappeared gradually from the urine; the result was not satisfactory.

Dr Scott Donkin has lately advocated the same treatment.*

Alcohol. It is well known that Bouchardat placed great confidence in this, in some shape or other, considering that it supplied the place of the hydrogen and carbon of the sugar; but, according to my experience, it requires to be given with great caution in those cases in which sugar in the urine depends upon the exaggerated healthy function of the liver; this, I have noticed, generally occurs at the commencement of Diabetes; after a time the irritation, which in such cases causes the disease, subsides and is followed by what Dr. Schiff calls paralysis, and therefore the treatment must be changed.

In those cases even in what is called the "irritative" form of the disease, where the patient has been in the habit of taking stimulants, generally it should be given, but much diluted, and in small quantities. The general health seems to require it or it flags, the spirits become much depressed, and I am sure in most cases less evil arises from giving, than from withholding, the alcohol. Where the disease arises from defective power, which I believe is the most frequent, alcohol in the shape of brandy, dry sherry, such as amontillado, and claret, does

* *The Lancet.* Nov. 27th, 1869.

good;* indeed I consider the bearing or not bearing stimulants a good diagnostic test of the two classes of Diabetes.

As far as diet is concerned, the great principle to be kept in view is to restrict the diet of the patient as little as possible consistent with the patient's welfare, and this for three reasons. 1st. By a diet as varied as possible you reduce to a minimum any probable injurious effect as far as the idiosyncrasies of patients are concerned. 2nd. You act up more to the physiological digestive structure of man midway in formation and complexity between that of herbivorous and carnivorous animals; nature designs his food to be a due mixture of nitrogenized and non-nitrogenised substances, and I need not say the more we are able to act up to such physiological indications the better it is. 3rd. We give more enjoyment to the patient and therefore little temptation to break through the rules laid down.

We must guard against loss of weight and power, and in those cases where a very strict regimen is required we must adopt it cautiously and slowly and not continue it too long; the plan above mentioned should be employed.

* Rum is much used in France; I have, however, never tried it.

We come now to the second point in the constitutional treatment, to which I attach the greatest importance, viz. Exercise. It is said in Germany that by well-regulated exercise alone has this disease been cured, and one writer, Düring of Amsterdam, attributes the benefit from taking Carlsbad water more, or at least as much, to the walking which the patient usually takes, when drinking the water; without going this length I am sure the advantage derived from exercise judiciously employed cannot be over-estimated. I believe, with M. Bouchardat, that it enables the system to utilize sugar that it could not otherwise do, and I am sure it thus enables the patient to be less restricted in his diet than he otherwise would have to be, and only by a diabetic patient can this advantage be duly appreciated. The exercise should be regularly sustained day by day, even in wet weather it should not be intermitted: of course great care should be taken against wet feet, and the shoes or boots ought to be changed in wet weather on returning home; it should never be carried to real fatigue, a feeling that exercise has been taken is the most that should be felt. Ten years ago when I was first siezed with an acute attack of Diabetes, and which threatened soon to end fatally, I became so weak and had so little muscular power that I could not walk 100 yards without great fatigue. The muscles of my legs were so powerless that I fell two or three times, and in going down the slightest slope I had to pay unusual attention to my legs or I was sure to fall. I began to take exercise regularly two or three times a day; wet or fine I took it. Gradually I gained strength so as to be able to walk five or six miles a day without fatigue. I now regularly walk from three to five or six miles a day.

Another case I have lately heard of is that of a gentleman who for two years noticed his mouth constantly dry and the saliva thick and gluey; one day the saliva appeared to him to have a sweetish taste; this immediately made him feel that he was labouring under Diabetes; on examining his urine he found a large quantity of sugar in it: he at once dieted himself, took gluten bread, and an entirely meat diet, with claret and Vichy water. This treatment was continued vigorously for several months; but not procuring any amelioration of his symptoms, he took ordinary bread, gave up Vichy water and took iodide of potassium; still not improving he took arsenic, four drops of liq. arsenicalis twice a day after his principal meals; this he continued for a month, at the end of which time he was no better; the quantity of sugar remained the same, the appetite was almost gone, he was rapidly becoming thinner and during the month he lost 50 lbs. in weight; his feebleness now was very great. He almost abandoned himself to despair. However, as he had hitherto led a sedentary life, he thought he would now change to an active one; at first he was able to walk a very short distance, at the end of two months he could walk about five miles a day; during his walk he began to perspire a little, this gradually increased: he confined his diet to beef and mutton, took ordinary bread, drank a bottle of vin ordinaire in the day and a bottle of Vichy water; he took coffee after each meal but abstained from all alcoholic liquor. His appetite soon improved, his strength returned, and the sugar began to diminish; from this time he gradually improved, and after six months he was well. He now recovered what he had lost in weight, his strength had completely returned and the sugar had entirely disappeared from the urine.

To carry into effect regular and sustained daily exercise requires great moral courage and energy, the langour and feeling of weakness are so great; but if the exercise be only carried out patiently and perseveringly the task will become not only more and more easy, but soon no longer a task but positively a pleasure.

I repeat, it must never be carried so far as to produce over-fatigue; we must ever remember there is a state of things in Diabetes that makes it difficult for the patient to recover from extra-fatigue, or from anything whatever that lowers his vital powers; we must be careful never to take too much out of a patient. And here I must caution a diabetic patient against taking long railway journeys. Whilst practising at Tunbridge Wells I saw two sudden deaths in diabetic patients after long journeys. One patient about two hours after his arrival from a journey of 200 miles was seized with vomiting. I saw him immediately, he was then in a half comatose state, pulse almost gone. Nothing stopped the vomiting, the patient became more and more comatose and died the same evening. The other patient, after a journey of 100 miles was also seized with vomiting, he became comatose and died within 24 hours of his arrival at Tunbridge Wells. Dr. Bence Jones cautions against long journeys and I am sure most wisely.

The recent observations of Fick and Wislicenius, on the result of a certain amount of work performed by themselves, point to the conclusion that muscular effort on a non-nitrogenous diet does not increase the quantity of urea excreted from the body; moreover they conclude that the oxidation of the quantity of albuminoid substance or plastic nitrogenous material which would correspond with the urea and other nitrogenous compounds then excreted, does not yield sufficient potential energy to perform the work accomplished. They ascended the Faulhorn, a mountain of the Bernese Oberland; they found that the ratio of work performed to the power derivable from the consumption of albuminoid substances in the body was as 3 to 1: they conclude therefore, since it is impossible for the oxidised albumen to be the sole and exclusive source of the power manifested in the work of the body, towards which it can contribute so little, that the oxidation of non-nitrogenous substances must yield at least the larger proportion of the force required, not only for the production of heat, but also of mechanical motion: finally they show that the resemblance of the living animal to a steam engine is more close than is usually admitted; the muscle is an apparatus for burning its appropriate fuel, the hydrocarbons and carbo-hydrates in the same manner as an engine burns its proper fuel, coal or coke: in action the muscle does not specially oxidise itself any more than the engine is burnt, but whilst in action both muscle and engine undergo wear.

The general conclusions of Fick and Wislicenius are strengthened by the subsequent researches of Dr. Frankland, who proves that in man non-nitrogenous substances must be the chief source of the energy which is transformed into muscular work, and that the muscle is an apparatus in which this energy is evolved at the expense of the hydro-carbonaceous fuel, or a machine for converting potential energy into mechanical force, and that it does not undergo much more waste when in action than when in comparative rest; though he admits that nitrogenous matter may be also employed for this purpose, as is illustrated by the work performed by men and animals fed on flesh diet exclusively, but it must be remembered that ordinary flesh contains much fatty matter. Liebig says carnivorous animals are always in motion, so necessary is it in order to decompose the muscles and the fat contained in them.* Here therefore we have explained physiologically, what we have learned practically—the advantages of exercise.

* Marshall's *Physiology*, vol. ii. p. 568—571.

Again, Dr. Parkes, in a paper read before the Royal Society of London, January 23rd, 1867, shewed that under every kind of food, whether azotised or non-azotised, muscular exertion was always accompanied by a diminution in the quantity of azotised substances eliminated by the kidneys. Also Winogradoff Bettrage* shewed this diminution, and that thus muscular activity depended on the hydrocarbons taken as food: he shewed likewise that in poisoning with curare, animals pass sugar in the urine, that in this form of poisoning two things are connected, paralysis of motion and the appearance of sugar in the urine; he therefore concludes that the muscles in motion destroy a notable quantity of sugar contained in the organism.

According to him also the lowering of the temperature is the result of this absence of combustion, here, agreeing with M. Bouchardat, and proving physiologically the advantage of exercise in Diabetes, not only by destroying sugar in the system, but also by allowing the patient to take bread without mischief, a boon which can only be sufficiently valued by one who has suffered from Diabetes. Exer-

* *Lehre von Diabetes Mellitus.* Virchow Archiv. Bd. 27. p. 553.

cise, as mentioned above, is to be short of fatigue, and for this reason, when a person is wearied less carbonic acid is exhaled: when taking exercise short of fatigue more carbonic acid is given off, and so more oxidisation of non-nitrogenous materials, such as sugar and fat, takes place. When walking, it is good, I am sure, to take occasionally deep inspirations so as to fill the lungs well, as Dr. E. Smith recommends. In early stages of Diabetes walking exercise is better than riding. Among the causes of Diabetes a sedentary life is particularly mentioned by writers.

The third point in constitutional treatment to which I attach very great importance is the warm bath. Sir Henry Marsh in his *Clinical Lectures* edited by Dr. H. Hughes, speaks favourably of their use. With me they seemed the turning-point of the disease. My skin was harsh, dry and unperspiring. I took one every other day at a temperature of 96° F., putting a tablespoonful of common washing soda into the water. I remained in the bath 15 minutes, brushing my skin well all the time so as to remove the oily matter which exists on the skin, and thus to render absorption more easy; being then very weak, I took it at 11·30 A.M., about two hours after breakfast. After three baths, the skin began to perspire slightly, and I shall never forget the relief I had to the dryness of the mouth and thirst. There seems to be that harmony of action, at least in Diabetes, between the cutaneous surface and mucous membrane of the mouth, that when the one acts the other does so also: from that time I have never felt thirst, though before the skin began to act I used to drink three or four tumblers of water, or milk and lime-water during the night. The frequency with which the baths ought to be taken greatly depends upon the strength of the patient: no weakness should be permitted to arise from their use. At the beginning a bath should be taken daily, or at least every other day: when the skin acts, once, or at most twice, a week is sufficient: of course in the intervening days the skin should be well washed, plenty of soap being used. If the patient can bear it the bath should be taken in the morning in summer, but in the forenoon in winter; whilst in the bath the skin should be exposed as much as possible to the sun's rays, for I am sure that light is most useful in promoting the action of the skin; we know its effects on plants. If the patient suffer from acidity, heartburn, sour eructations, or if the saliva when first secreted be acid as shown by litmus paper, the soda bath may be taken every day or every other day according to its effects and the strength of the patient.

That the soda penetrates into the system especially if the skin be well brushed whilst in the bath is proved by the experiments of Petit.* I know the absorption of any medicinal substance by the skin has been denied but I think wrongly. Two great powers in promoting absorption are first to scrub the skin well whilst in the bath so as to remove all oily matter. Secondly, that the solution should be very weak, of lower specific gravity than that of the blood, so that endosmosis may take place: the average specific gravity of the blood, according to Nasse, may be fixed at 1055. I may here remark that in rheumatic and gouty cases I have found the alkaline bath not only useful during an attack, but also in warding one off. I have had three patients who were martyrs to rheumatism, and two to gout, and who, since using this bath twice a week, have not had a single attack for years. I need not say that in such cases, if albumen be present in the urine and the reaction is alkaline or nearly so, such a bath should not be used. I find an alkali introduced into the

* *Des Eaux Minereaux de Vichy.*

system by the skin does not weaken the digestive organs.

Fourth point. Warm clothing. Winter and summer the patient should be enveloped in flannel. In winter a flannel binder should also be worn round the abdomen. The patient should not sleep in the flannel worn during the day; but should change it at night for another: when taken off they should be thoroughly exposed to the air.

Thus far for the constitutional treatment: and now we come to medicine. On entering upon the medical treatment of Diabetes we cannot but wonder at the numerous drugs that have been recommended. Much difficulty arises from this. Frank recognised it, when he said "Nullibi plerumque medicina auxilii tam egena est quam ubi majores remediorum divitias pro unâ eâdemque ægritudine possidere gloriantur theorici; in ipso Diabete tam multa tamque contraria inter se auxilia lucidata fuerunt, ut vel eâ hâc solâ rationis medendi inconstantiâ plurimorum jam nimis manifestetur inertia." In fact there is hardly a medicine in the Pharmacopœia that has not been used, and what is extraordinary too, used with success. Nothing I think tends to prove more that Diabetes is most frequently a functional, in opposition to an organic, disease; for it seems impossible that if it were the latter such success could take place. In the prescribing of drugs, I take as my basis the two established principles in all true cases of Diabetes; these are too few red corpuscles in the blood, and too little oxygen consumed by the patient. The former is not only proved experimentally, but is seen in the pale face, lips, and inner lining membrane of the mouth, or if the patient should have a florid complexion, (it arises from congested veins, which are often seen much enlarged, and the face of a bluish tint, especially in cold weather,) the lips &c. are usually paler than they ought to be. To remedy this first defect I use some preparation of iron, usually the tincture of the perchloride in small doses, four to five drops for a male, two to three for a female, with one or two drops of tincture of nux vomica, and chlorate of potash, eight to ten grains for a male, five to seven for a female, three times a day. The chlorate of potash I add on the theory that the salt is decomposed in the system, and gives off its oxygen, and thus aids in making up for the diminished absorption of oxygen, and so fulfilling the second indication: whether I am thus right in prescribing these drugs or not, I am sure there is no combination from which I have derived more benefit than this. This prescription I employ when the disease seems to arise from an exaggerated sugar-producing function of the liver. When the Diabetes seems to arise from want of power, and this in the beginning, I order citrate of iron, two grains for a male, and one for a female, with the above mentioned quantity of chlorate of potash, and half a drachm of aromatic spirits of ammonia, three times a day. The great object is to avoid all irritation, and as it were to insinuate the medicine into the system; it must be continued for a long time; I took it for four months, with the steady continuance of the constitutional treatment above mentioned, before I got clear of sugar in the urine.

There is no more suitable way for a patient to take iron than drinking the Tunbridge Wells water. From the middle of May to the middle of October, in ordinary seasons, the waters may be drunk. This water is perfectly transparent, giving out no air bubbles, its taste is strongly chalybeate; when taken at the Wells it has an agreeable freshness. Its temperature is always, summer or winter, between 50° and 52° F. The quantity of water yielded by the spring, for there is only one, though there are two basins, one being filled by the overflowing of the other, generally remains the same throughout the year: it is not affected by wet or dry seasons, even during the last summer (1870) the spring yielded its usual quantity of water: about February, when the land-springs break, there is a considerable increase in the quantity, but how much has never been estimated. Its constituents are chloride of sodium, sulphate of soda, lime, protoxide of iron, manganese, silica; also three gases, carbonic acid, oxygen, and nitrogen: it owes its celebrity to the iron which it contains: the quantity is exceedingly small, not above ·14 grains in half a pint, yet the water requires to be taken with great caution. During a long practice at Tunbridge Wells I found medical men at a distance, from the small quantity of iron which the water contains, prescribed it in far too large doses, deranged stomach and headache being the result. Whilst taking the water great attention is required to be paid to the digestive organs: the bowels ought on no account to be confined, one free action at least ought to be secured daily, but purging should be sedulously avoided. If the patient be strong enough, the water should be taken in the morning, and at the well; on no account should it be carried away and drunk at home, and this for two reasons, the quantity of carbonic acid gas is small, there being only a surplus of a grain to keep the iron in solution, so that the escape of a very small amount of the gas causes a precipitation of the iron, and the water loses its virtue; the second reason is that the patient should walk after drinking the water, as it promotes digestion. He should be at the wells about 7. 30 or 8 A.M., and begin by taking the smallest glass, two ounces of water, (there are three glasses in use, the smallest two ounces, the next four ounces, the third six ounces;) he should then walk for a quarter of an hour, then take another glass and walk for another quarter of an hour: on reaching home he should rest a little, say half an hour, before taking breakfast. On the third day he should begin afternoon doses, commencing about 3 A.M., taking two of the same glasses with the quarter of an hour walk between, and then walking a quarter of an hour after the second glass. If this quantity produces no indigestion, no feeling of weight at stomach, or headache, he should continue the same quantity for a week; if bad symptoms arise he ought at once to see one of the medical gentlemen of the town, and be guided by him as to his mode of procedure. After a week, if there be nothing to contra-indicate it, another small glass may be added both morning and afternoon, with the quarter of an hour interval of walking. This may be continued as long as the patient remains at the Wells, if no bad symptoms arise: the patient should not leave off taking the waters on his own responsibility. Before beginning to take the water it is well to be three or four days in the place. Before getting up in the morning, a tumbler of milk with a teaspoonful of brandy may be taken, and a little of the bread or cakes mentioned under diet: if it produce acidity or weight at stomach, two tablespoonfuls of lime water may be added. If the patient be not strong enough to take the water in the morning, he should commence about eleven o'clock, or two hours after breakfast, proceeding exactly in the same way as before described. In taking iron I never give it in such doses as to render the stools very black, I consider a slight tinge is enough: when the stools are very black, it shows more iron is being taken than can be assimilated, and it may thus become a source of irritation. The rule for its use is, very small doses diluted largely, rendering the solution of less specific gravity than the blood, so that rapid endosmosis may take place, enabling the iron to be quickly assimilated. The colour of the stools may be regarded as a good test as to the dose to be given; if it produces very black motions the dose must be diminished. I believe the principle of small doses, so as to avoid irritation when the medicine is given for a long time, is too much lost sight of in the treatment of all chronic diseases. If the patient's symptoms indicate much acidity, in addition to the water and baths the following draught may be taken two hours after breakfast, and luncheon, and at bedtime,

Rec. Potassæ Bicarbonatis ℈j.
Ammoniæ Carbonatis grs. iv.
Tr. Calumbæ ʒj,
Tr. Nucis Vomicæ ♏j.
Aquæ ad. ℥iss :

but as soon as the acid symptoms are removed, this should be given up. I order it at the time mentioned that the acidity after stomachic digestion may be neutralized. With the use of alkaline baths I find it very rare to be obliged to use this mixture long. As soon as the symptoms from acidity are removed, I reduce the bicarbonate of potash one half, and after two days give it up, returning to it if needful.

The taking of fatty matter in some form is

important. The loss of so much carbon and hydrogen as are contained in the sugar excreted cannot but interfere with the nutrition of the body, consequently the supply of carbon and hydrogen in the shape of fat must be beneficial. As a general rule, therefore, fat ought to be given in large quantities, and in as pleasant a form as possible. Cod liver oil, when it agrees, may be given, if not, as much cream or fresh butter as can be digested. I eat a very large quantity of good fresh butter, and have found great benefit from doing so. All physicians are agreed as to the good to be derived from taking fatty matter: in looking over my notes of cases I find that many of my Diabetic patients have had a dislike to fat, and therefore have eaten but little, agreeing in this respect with many consumptive patients. When the patient is sleepless, or restless, at night, I order pil opii. grain i. or grains ij. at bedtime; except for this purpose, I never employ opium. I tried it on myself in large doses, as I have tried almost every medicine that has been recommended with any authority, but found mischief from it. The urine was reduced from seventy-six ounces to thirty-two ounces: the specific gravity was 1054 instead of 1036; on boiling it with liq. potassæ the urine became very dark:

I felt so ill and heartless that I had not resolution to make out the quantity of sugar it contained.

Difference of opinion exists as to the quantity of fluid a Diabetic patient may take—how far such an one should drink to abate the thirst that prevails. Some consider it well to limit the fluid that should be taken, in fact that the patient should suffer inconvenience from thirst. I dare not adopt this plan, but have generally allowed the patient to allay his thirst so as to suffer as little as possible from it; but in doing so I order ice or iced water, the latter to be drunk slowly, and to be kept, and moved about in the mouth for some time before being swallowed. All gulping down of fluids should be avoided; by this manner of acting it is extraordinary what relief is obtained. With regard to the stimulating drink that should be allowed, I permit brandy, dry sherries, such as amontillado, and claret. I generally order the wines to be diluted, even the claret.

Drinking the waters of Vichy has been much recommended in the cure of Diabetes. The following is my experience: I was at Vichy two successive years and have had two friends (Diabetics) there. The good results derived from the thermal baths are manifest at the time; the benefit however, was not permanent. It is difficult to say how much depends on the use of the baths and drinking the water, as there are so many other beneficial causes in operation, such as change of climate, of scenery, alteration in living &c., the walking exercise that is enforced; that all these have something to do with the improvement that takes place at Vichy is rendered more probable from the fact, that whatever may be the place to which a diabetic patient may go there is generally an improvement in health at first. In all the diabetic patients who came to Tunbridge Wells an improvement was observed before treatment had been adopted, except in the two cases before mentioned, who died after a long railway journey.

There are many springs at Vichy, but the characters of them are very much alike. Carbonate of soda is the chief constituent, then in smaller quantities carbonate of lime and magnesia, and in still smaller quantities, chloride and sulphate of soda, oxide of iron, iodine and bromine; there is a small quantity of nitrogen and a considerable quantity of carbonic acid gas so as to render the water sparkling; this is most marked in the Celestin spring. The temperature varies; the following is that of the chief springs as taken by M. Petit in May, 1846.

The Grande Grille	32°C	or	89·6°F
Puits Chomel	40°C	„	104°F
Grand Puits Carré	45°C	„	113°F
Hôpital	32°C	„	89·6°F
Lucas	28°C	„	82·4°F
Celéstin	15°C	„	59°F

The Celestin is the coldest and most pleasant to drink.

I was at Vichy in 1865 and 1866. The first time I went in May, here I joined a friend who was also suffering from Diabetes. I had now been ill for four years; my symptoms were little or no thirst, a perspiring skin, pulse weak, averaging about 90, stomach much deranged, with great acidity, sour eructations and burning pains: the saliva acid, even when first secreted. I was very weak especially in my legs, the quantity of urine in 24 hours 79 oz., specific gravity 1040, strongly acid; after fermentation, specific gravity 1024, showing a loss of 16 degrees, and indicating 1264 grains of sugar in the 24 hours; this was the average amount of sugar passed during the week before I went to Vichy. I was on the following diet: meat, green vegetables, cakes made from Dr. Camplin's flour (I had not relaxed my diet then), a tablespoonful of brandy in a tumbler of water with half a bottle of Vichy water at luncheon and dinner, tea and milk; the fluid taken in the twenty-four hours, about four quarts. I had an opportunity of examining my friend's urine before going to Vichy; its specific gravity was 1031, quantity in twenty-four hours 100 oz., after fermentation specific gravity was 1019, the loss being 12 degrees, showing 1200 grains of sugar in twenty-four hours: the symptoms were considerable thirst, dry skin, great weakness and little power to walk, appetite deficient. We both consulted Dr. Willemain at Vichy, who continued the same diet, with Bouchardat's gluten bread; we were to drink of the Grande Grille water 2 oz. at 7·30 A.M. then walk for half an hour; then 2 oz. at 8 and another walk for half an hour; then 2 oz. at 8·30 and walk for 40 minutes; then take a bath at a temperature of 95°F remaining in it for 20 minutes. At 3 P.M. we were again to take 2 oz. of water, walk for half an hour and then take 2 oz. of water. This was continued for 10 days. The effect of the treatment was remarkable. The quantity of sugar in my urine was greatly diminished (it was determined in both cases by M. Jaurand, an excellent and obliging chemist); it was only 315 grains in twenty-four hours, urine slightly alkaline, amount 60 oz.; the quantity of sugar passed by my friend was 400 grains in twenty-four hours, specific gravity 1019, urine slightly acid, amount 66 oz.; the appetite was much improved and the skin was moist.

For the next twenty-one days the same diet, baths, &c., were continued, except that we drank in the afternoon the water from "Celestin" at 3 and 3·30. At the end of this time the following were the conditions of the patients: I had become thinner, having lost 14 lbs. in weight, no thirst, perspiring freely, pulse 74 stronger, quantity of urine in twenty-four hours 66 oz. specific gravity 1015 slightly acid, sugar 63 grains only in twenty-four hours, spirits depressed, much more feeble, appetite not voracious, but thoroughly enjoyed food. My friend was also thinner, appetite not good, perspiring freely, very acid. Urine in twenty-four hours 69 oz., specific gravity 1012 slightly alkaline; sugar in twenty-four hours 80 grains. I had taken no medicine; my friend took sp. ammoniæ aromaticæ, tr. aurantiæ aa ʒss twice a day. My friend and I then left Vichy.

On reaching home I continued the same diet, eating the gluten bread as at Vichy, and drinking four glasses of claret during the day. I resumed practice, but refused all night work; at the end of a month I found general symptoms as follows: no thirst, perspiring freely, appetite very fair, quantity of urine in twenty-four hours 60 oz. being disturbed about three times during the night, specific gravity 1035 very acid, amount of sugar, 713 grains. During the summer, autumn and winter I kept very well, the urine, in all respects, remaining about the same.

I may say of my friend, whom I have frequently seen, and who has been taking by my direction, twice a week, a bath with soda, as described above, that the diabetic symptoms are quite in abeyance and though sugar is still in the urine (1870) it has never exceeded 300 grains in the 24 hours, the specific gravity ranges between 1025 and 1035, the quantity about 60 ounces in the 24 hours.

I went to Vichy for the second time in May, 1866, and stayed 21 days, pursuing the same treatment as before. The result was the same with regard to the diminution both in the quantity of urine passed and in the sugar it contained; urine was now 58 oz. in twenty-four hours, sugar 50 grains. I was much thinner and considerably depressed in spirits and had lost muscular power.

I have been minute in describing my case, because I am sure I was wrong in drinking so much water and taking a bath every day; as no symptoms of acidity were present after my visit to Vichy and as my muscular power was not very great, daily baths were not needed; one once or at the most twice a week would have been sufficient.

I have sent several patients to Vichy and have prescribed the thermal treatment carefully, attending particularly to this, and using the water and baths accordingly. When the urine is alkaline or nearly so, and the perspiration, which I may say always follows the bath, is not very acid, a bath every other day is enough and less water should be drunk; the great object is to avoid depressed spirits or weakness from the treatment.

I relate another case, shewing that in a very advanced stage of the disease, the water and baths may be used with advantage, if great care be taken. Last year, a lady, suffering from Diabetes went by my direction to Vichy; she had had sugar in her urine for about 20 years, but until the last year the general symptoms had not been very severe; she was 64 years of age: the average amount of urine passed in twenty-four hours was 60 oz. specific gravity 1029, sugar about 11 grains in the ounce; she perspired freely; she complained of a dry mouth; her appetite was moderate; she was suffering from cataract; she complained much of acidity, and was very subject to diarrhœa, she remained at Vichy three weeks; I ordered a bath three time a week, to drink 4 oz. in two doses from the Grande Grille in the morning with a walk for half an hour between the doses, and the same quantity taken in like manner, from Celestin in the afternoon. She took ordinary bread, on account of the tendency to diarrhœa, green vegetables and vin ordinaire. She returned improved. The urine reduced to about 46 oz. specific gravity 1035, quantity of sugar in twenty-four hours 200 grains, thirst and acidity gone.

I have seen three patients who not only did not benefit from going to Vichy but actually returned worse; they were all young, that is to say, under 32 years of age. There was a history of consumption in each case; in two commencing consolidation of the apex of left lung, thus countenancing the opinion of Dr. Durand Fardel a physician at Vichy, that the least predisposition to pulmonary phthisis is a contra-indication to the use of Vichy waters.

I say nothing about the waters of Carlsbad, as I have not been there, but as they combine purgative qualities with alkaline, their action is easily comprehended, they will of course be contra-indicated when there is a tendency to diarrhœa, or when there is great exhaustion: greater care will be required in their use than in those of Vichy.

Professor Seeger* says they overcome the most troublesome symptoms of Diabetes, such as the dryness of the mouth, the excessive thirst, and the frequency of micturition. In 100 cases he observed, there were only 10 or 12 in which these effects were not produced. In the others the sugar disappeared from the urine.

Dr. Crozant, who practises at Pougues a town situated on the great road between Paris and Lyons, about 9 miles from Nevers, speaks highly of the waters there. They contain carbonate of magnesia, lime, and iron, and are very gaseous, having about 325·9 cubic inches of carbonic acid gas in the imperial gallon. He considers that they regulate the function of the liver. He has treated many cases of Diabetes, and with remarkable success. It appears from him that the waters are most useful when there is evidence of congestion of the liver. I have not been to Pougues, nor have I seen a patient who has been there.

In Diabetes there is usually much acidity from derangement of the digestive organs; the urine also is very acid.

* *Arch. Gen. de Medecin*, 6th series, 1867, vol. ix, p. 295.

Alkalies, either in the form of natural waters as Vichy, or medicine, or baths, should be given, so as to neutralize the acidity, and by doing so it is remarkable how in all cases the quantity of water as well as sugar is diminished; but unless other treatment is adopted so as to give tone to the system, the benefit is only temporary. It is admitted by many, if not by all physicians at Vichy, that tonics should be taken with the waters, and with this I fully concur. Dr. Durand Fardel draws the following conclusion from 122 cases treated by him at Vichy. First. That cures are exceptional. Second. That relapses are frequent, but in general not severe, and in a good number of cases an arrest of the disease takes place, in which the patient maintains a state of health very comfortable and compatible with the exigencies of life, if not pursuing very fatiguing occupations; he adds undoubtedly the course of the disease has not always been satisfactory; and further that the thermic treatment with careful dieting and tonic medicines is the most efficacious.

The alkaline bath, prepared as directed under the heading of baths, is, as I have before said, the most effectual remedy, but when there are no symptoms of acidity it must be used with caution, though it will always be borne once, if not twice, a week: no debility must be produced either by baths or alkaline medicines.

After my return from Vichy the second time I recommenced practice: the sugar again increased, but not to any very great amount, the general symptoms, however, as thirst, dryness of skin, did not return. During the next three years I had much anxiety and had to work very hard in my practice, yet by taking 2 or 3 courses of Tunbridge Wells water during the year and regular exercise I kept myself wonderfully well; occasionally when I had unusual anxiety there was a return of the dryness of mouth, &c., slight increase in the quantity of urine as well as of the sugar in it. Towards the end of 1868 as sugar still continued, about 4 grains to the ounce, quantity of urine about 50 ounces, increased by anxiety to 7 grains in the ounce and 60 or 70 ounces of urine, I determined to retire for a year or two from active practice and endeavour, if possible, to get entirely free from sugar. For 3 months, I took no medicine, living on wheat meal bread, meat, vegetables, and drinking claret: I remained stationary as far as sugar was concerned. I then tried inhalation of oxygen, twice a day for two months, but derived no benefit. I next tried the peroxide of hydrogen, as recommended by Dr. B. Richardson, for 3 months, but was no better. I then determined to take tincture of perchloride of iron, and chlorate of potash; to continue to walk regularly and persistently every day; to wash all my body daily with lukewarm water, using plenty of soap, and exposing my body as much as possible to the sun; to take a soda bath twice a week, and to clothe in flannel. After 3 months I was free from sugar, and have been so ever since.

In two other cases in which the same treatment has been carried out the patients are much improved; the symptoms in both were very severe, dry skin, parched mouth, great feebleness, increased quantity of urine; in the one ninety ounces in twenty-four hours, specific gravity 1042, sugar 2840 grains a day: in the other, urine 76 ounces, sp. gr. 1040, sugar 1292 grains. The first used a soda bath every other day, as there was considerable acidity of stomach and rather severe dyspeptic symptoms, took half a bottle of soda water with half a bottle of Vichy water at luncheon, and the same amount at dinner. The second, as there were no symptoms of acidity and was also very weak, took a bath once a week, and Vichy water with an equal quantity of soda water and a tablespoonful of brandy twice a day. Both were allowed four glasses of claret during the day. The improvement in both is remarkable, though they have been under treatment but a short time; the one two months, the other six weeks. The skin is perspiring, all dryness of mouth is gone, both are much stronger and walk better, one about 1½ miles a day without fatigue, the other a mile. The urine of the first, sixty-five ounces, specific gravity 1028, sugar two grains in the ounce; of the second, sixty-two ounces, specific gravity 1024, sugar twelve grains in the ounce. I have no doubt that by continuing this treatment both will get well.

The treatment must be strictly carried out in detail: for instance, without walking I am sure the relaxation of diet recommended by me could not be adopted without mischief, and so the walking exercise allows more variety of food, and often even, when circumstances demand it, permits farinaceous aliment to be taken without detriment.

I believe that Diabetes in most cases is a functional disease, and that therefore it is curable: that cases will occur that will prove fatal under any treatment cannot be doubted, when we consider that the general symptoms of Diabetes, as well as sugar in the urine are associated with, if not dependent upon, such diseases as those described by Dr. Dickinson* of Cambridge.

In conclusion; the symptoms and effects of Diabetes point it out as being a very complex disease, the cause of which may often escape us; the presence of sugar in the urine constituting, not the morbid state, but only a symptom. It requires therefore great patience and perseverance in the treatment, and the principles of treatment must be modified according to each individual case; and how can it be otherwise when we consider what we have to deal with, how age, sex, temperament, and previous habit modify the effects of regimen and medicine, and how these are further modified by other forces that come into operation?

* *Transactions of the Medical and Chirurgical Society.* Vol. liii.

London: Printed by H. K. Lewis, 136 Gower Street, W.C.

NEW BOOKS

PUBLISHED AND SOLD BY

H. K. LEWIS, 136 GOWER STREET. W.C.

Dr. FELIX Von NIEMEYER.

*A Text Book of Practical Medicine, with particular refer-*ENCE TO PHYSIOLOGY AND PATHOLOGICAL ANATOMY. Translated from the Seventh German Edition, by special permission of the Author, by GEORGE H. HUMPHREYS, M.D., and CHARLES E. HACKLEY, M.D. 2 vols. large 8vo. 36s.

"The publication of these volumes brings within the reach of the busy practitioner, the student, and the teacher in our schools, one of the best text-books in any language. As the translators say, 'Professor Niemeyer's volumes present a concise and well-digested epitome of the results of ten years of carefully rendered clinical observation by the most illustrious medical authorities of Europe,' elaborated, we may add, by a most able teacher and an experienced physician. . . . Not the least valuable part of the book will be found in the therapeutical sections, and the numerous formulæ, which are given most clearly, will prove a boon to many a hardworked practitioner."—*Brit. and For. Med. Chir. Review.*

"The task of a reviewer is an easy and glorious one in noticing such a work as this. It is at once comprehensive and concise; it is characterised by clearness and originality and it differs from many German works on Medicine in the sagacious appreciation of the value of therapeutics which is manifested by the author . . . . We can cordially recommend the work as one from the perusal of which every physician may derive profit, which will be found replete with information of direct practical value, and which is instinct with a spirit of candid and earnest inquiry, which is worthy of all praise. The translation on the whole, is very creditably performed, and the volumes are handsomely brought out."—*Dublin Quarterly Journal of Med. Science.*

DR. THEODOR BILLROTH.

Professor of Surgery, Vienna.

General Surgical Pathology and Therapeutics, in fifty Lectures, A text-book for Students and Physicians. Translated from the fourth German edition, with special permission of the author, by C. E. HACKLEY, M.A., M.D. 18s.

Dr. SYDNEY RINGER.

Professor of Therapeutics in University College.

A Hand-book of Therapeutics. Small 8vo. 10s 6d.

"The work contains a large amount of most useful matter, much of which will be novel to the English student. There is moreover an honest directness of statement, and an apparent desire to balance opposing opinions with candour, which is calculated to attract confidence. We can scarcely doubt that the present edition will be quickly sold."—*The Practitioner.*

Dr. J. WICKHAM LEGG,

Assist. Physician to St. Bartholomew's Hospital. &c.

*A Guide to the Examination of the Urine; intended chief*ly for Clinical Clerks and Students. Second Edit., revised and enlarged, fcap. 8vo, cl. 2s. 6d.

"We are glad to welcome this little work. . . Just what was wanted."—*British Med. Journal.*

"This little work forms a concise guide to the complete 'clinical' examination of the urine. . . The work is a very handy one, and we recommend the student to make it his companion in the wards of the hospital."—*Lancet*, Jan. 8th, 1870.

SIR W. JENNER, BART., M.D.

The Practical Medicine of To-day: Two Addresses delivered before the British Medical Association, and the Epidemiological Society. Small 8vo. cloth, 1s 6d.

DR. C. F. OLDHAM.

Assistant Surgeon H.M. Indian Forces. Fellow of the Royal Medical and Chirurgical Society. Late in Medical charge of Dalhousie Sanitarium.

*What is Malaria? and why is it most intense in Hot Cli*MATES? An Explanation of the Nature and Cause of the so-called Marsh Poison, with the Principles to be observed for the preservation of Health in Tropical Climates and Malarious Districts. 8vo. 7s. 6d.

DR. ALFRED VOGEL.

*A Practical Treatise on the Diseases of Children. Trans*lated and edited by H. RAPHAEL, M.D. From the fourth German Edition, illustrated by six lithographic plates, part coloured, large 8vo, 600 pages, 18s.

"Several excellent lithographic plates, and the admirable way in which the volume is got up, add to the attractiveness of Dr. Vogel's work. Dr. Vogel is more a physician than a surgeon; and he is clearly a physician of no mean order, judged either from a pathological or a clinical standpoint. When he treats a subject exhaustively he produces an essay, clear yet elaborate, which inspires the reader with confidence that the author believed himself to have the best possible reasons for all that he says. Of Dr. Vogel, as a medical practitioner, we would only say that he seems to belong to the comparatively small class of physicians who, when they give a medicine, have a clear notion of the effects which they desire it to produce."—*Brit. Med. Journal.*

JOSEPH TOYNBEE, F.R.S.

The Diseases of the Ear: Their Diagnosis and Treatment. Demy 8vo, 8s. 6d. With Supplement by JAMES HINTON.

"Great credit is due to Mr. HINTON for the manner in which he has supplemented the labours of his deceased friend. The work in its new form constitutes a most reliable guide to the treatment of aural disease, and is without a rival in the English language."—LANCET.

The mantle of the master has fallen upon a worthy successor, and in the hands of its present accomplished editor the volume will maintain its high position as the first text-book on the bject"—*Med. Times & Gazette.*

DR. THOMAS INMAN.

Physician to the Royal Infirmary, Liverpool, &c.

On the Restoration of Health. Demy 8vo, cloth, 7s 6d.

"It would be unfair to deny that Dr. Inman often makes some pithy remarks, and that though as a general rule, he is needlessly aggressive and uncharitable to his brother practitioners, his criticisms are occasionally as just as they are vigorous. His remarks on myalgia are well worthy of attention......Some of his remarks on pathology and treatment are worthy of attention, as coming from an experienced physician of a sceptical and inquiring turn of mind."—*Edin. Med. Journal*, Feb. 1871.

On the Preservation of Health. Second Edit. Demy 8vo, 5s.

DR. HORACE DOBELL.

On Diet and Regimen in Sickness and Health, and on the Interdependence and Prevention of Diseases and the diminution of their fatality. Fourth Edition, rewritten and much enlarged, sm. 8vo, cloth, 3s. 6d.

The Nursing Schedule. To be used in Fevers, Inflammations, Surgical Cases, and other acute Illnesses. In packets reporting 14 days and 14 nights. 1s.

DR. MORITZ MEYER.

Electricity in its relation to Practical Medicine. Translated from the third German Edition, with notes and additions by WILLIAM A. HAMMOND, M.D. With illustrations, large 8vo, 500 pages, cloth, 18s.

"The number of editions through which Dr. Meyer's work has passed in Germany attest the esteem in which it is there held, and we do not doubt that an equal measure of approbation will be accorded to it in this country."—*Dublin Quarterly Journal of Med. Science.*

DR. CHARLES A. GORDON.

Deputy Inspector General of Hospitals, Army Medical Department.

Remarks on Army Surgeons and their works. Demy 8vo, 5s.

SPENCER WATSON.

Surgeon to the Great Northern and the Central London Ophthalmic Hospital

On Abscess and Tumours of the Orbit. 8vo, 6s.

DRS. MEIGS and PEPPER.

A Practical Treatise on the Diseases of Children. By Dr. J. FORSYTH MEIGS, M.D., Fellow of the College of Physicians of Philadelphia, etc., etc., and WILLIAM PEPPER, M.D., Physician to the Philadelphia Hospital, etc., etc. Fourth Edition, roy. 8vo, cloth, cut edges, pp. 920, 26s.

"There is but little to find fault with compared with what there is to praise, and perhaps if we had said all we felt we might endanger the value of our praise by over-laudation. It is the most complete work on the subject in our language; it contains at once the results of personal observation and the experience of others; its quotations from the most recent authorities, both home and foreign, are ample; and we think the authors deserve congratulation for having produced a book unequalled for the use of the student, and indispensable as a work of reference for the practitioner."—*American Journal of the Medical Sciences*, Oct. 1870.

"It is a work of more than 900 good American pages, and is more encyclopædial than clinical. But it is clinical, and withal most effectually brought up to the light, pathological and therapeutical, of the present day...... The thoroughly fresh nature of the book is seen in the care with which certain articles have been written. Such are those on Rickets and Tuberculosis, Infantile Atrophic Paralysis, and Progressive Paralysis. We are glad to add this work to our library. There are few diseases of children which it does not treat of fully and wisely in the light of the latest physiololgical pathological, and therapeutical science."—*Lancet.*

DR. J. C. THOROWGOOD.

The Climatic Treatment of Consumption and Chronic LUNG DISEASES. Third Edition, post 8vo, cloth, 3s. 6d.

DR. S. SCOTT ALISON.

*Morbid Conditions of the Throat, in their relation to Pul-*MONARY CONSUMPTION. Post 8vo, 3s. 6d.

MEREDITH REDMAN.

Human Anatomy: forming a complete series of Questions and Answers for the use of Medical Students. 2 vols., 12mo, cloth, price 10s. 6d.

DR. W. F. MONTGOMERY.

Late Professor of Midwifery at King's and Queen's College of Physicians, Ireland, etc., etc.

An Exposition of the Signs and Symptoms of Pregnancy: with some other papers on subjects connected with Midwifery. Coloured plates. Second Edition, 8vo, cloth, (12s 6d. net,) pub. 25s.

DR. ABBOTTS SMITH.

On Human Entozoa and the Disorders produced by Worms. With numerous Engravings and a Glossary of Terms, demy 8vo, 5s. pp. 257.

JOSEPH SAMPSON GAMGEE.

*On the Advantages of the Starched Apparatus in the Treat-*MENT OF FRACTURES AND DISEASES OF JOINTS. Being the First Part of an Essay to which the Council of University College Awarded the Liston Clinical Medal. Demy 8vo, cloth, with illustrations, 5s.

DR. JOHN COCKLE, M.A.

Physician to the Royal Free Hospital.

On Intra-Thoracic Cancer. 8vo, 4s. 6d.

DR. GRAILY HEWITT.

Professor of Midwifery and Diseases of Women in University College.

Outlines of Pictorial Diagnosis of Diseases of Women. 4to, 6s.

ALEXANDER BRUCE.

Observations in the Military Hospitals of Dresden. 8vo, 1s.

An Epitome of the Veneral Diseases, being a succinct account of the well established and more important facts relating to these diseases. 12mo, 1s.

C. H. F. ROUTH.

*On the Cheapest and most Nutritious Food for Chari-*TABLE INSTITUTIONS AND THE POOR: Being the Result of an Inquiry, made by desire, on the Food supplied to the Hill Street Female Refuge. 1s.

J. H. GRIESBACH.

ANALYSIS OF MUSICAL SOUNDS with illustrative figures of the ratios of vibrations of musical intervals and their compounds, temperament, harmonic vibration, resultant sounds, &c. &c. Small folio, cloth, £1 5s.